TAÏ

The Little Samurai

Wild Animals!

#5

SMOOCH
SMACK
SMOCK

Laurent R...
illustrated by **Nicolas Ryser**
Translation: **Edward Gauvin**

GRAPHIC UNIVERSE™ • MINNEAPOLIS

STORY BY LAURENT RICHARD
ILLUSTRATIONS BY NICOLAS RYSER
TRANSLATION BY EDWARD GAUVIN

FIRST AMERICAN EDITION PUBLISHED IN 2014 BY GRAPHIC UNIVERSE™.

NEM PAS MAL! BY LAURENT RICHARD AND NICOLAS RYSER © BAYARD ÉDITIONS, 2011
COPYRIGHT © 2014 BY LERNER PUBLISHING GROUP, INC., FOR THE US EDITION

GRAPHIC UNIVERSE™ IS A TRADEMARK OF LERNER PUBLISHING GROUP, INC.

GRAPHIC UNIVERSE™
A DIVISION OF LERNER PUBLISHING GROUP, INC.
241 FIRST AVENUE NORTH
MINNEAPOLIS, MN 55401 USA

FOR READING LEVELS AND MORE INFORMATION,
LOOK UP THIS TITLE AT WWW.LERNERBOOKS.COM.

MAIN BODY TEXT SET IN CCWILDWORDS 8.5/10.5.
TYPEFACE PROVIDED BY FONTOGRAPHER.

LIBRARY OF CONGRESS CATALOGING-IN-PUBLICATION DATA

RICHARD, LAURENT, 1968-
    [NEM PAS MAL! ENGLISH]
    WILD ANIMALS! / BY LAURENT RICHARD ; ILLUSTRATED BY NICOLAS RYSER ; TRANSLATION:
    EDWARD GAUVIN. — FIRST AMERICAN EDITION.
        P.   CM. — (TAO, THE LITTLE SAMURAI ; #5)
    SUMMARY: TRAINING AT MASTER SNOW'S DOJO TAKES A TWIST WHEN NEW STUDENT RUBY
    ARRIVES AND DISTRACTS SOME OF THE STUDENTS FROM THEIR PRACTICE, WHICH NOW INCLUDES
    WORKING WITH ANIMALS.
    ISBN 978-1-4677-2098-4 (LIB. BDG. : ALK. PAPER)
    ISBN 978-1-4677-4662-5 (EBOOK)
    1. GRAPHIC NOVELS. [1. GRAPHIC NOVELS. 2. MARTIAL ARTS—FICTION. 3. SAMURAI—FICTION.
    4. ZOO ANIMALS—FICTION.] I. RYSER, NICOLAS, ILLUSTRATOR. II. GAUVIN, EDWARD, TRANSLATOR.
    III. TITLE.
    PZ7.7.RSWIL 2014
    741.5'944—DC23   2013038070

MANUFACTURED IN THE UNITED STATES OF AMERICA
1 - VI - 7/15/14

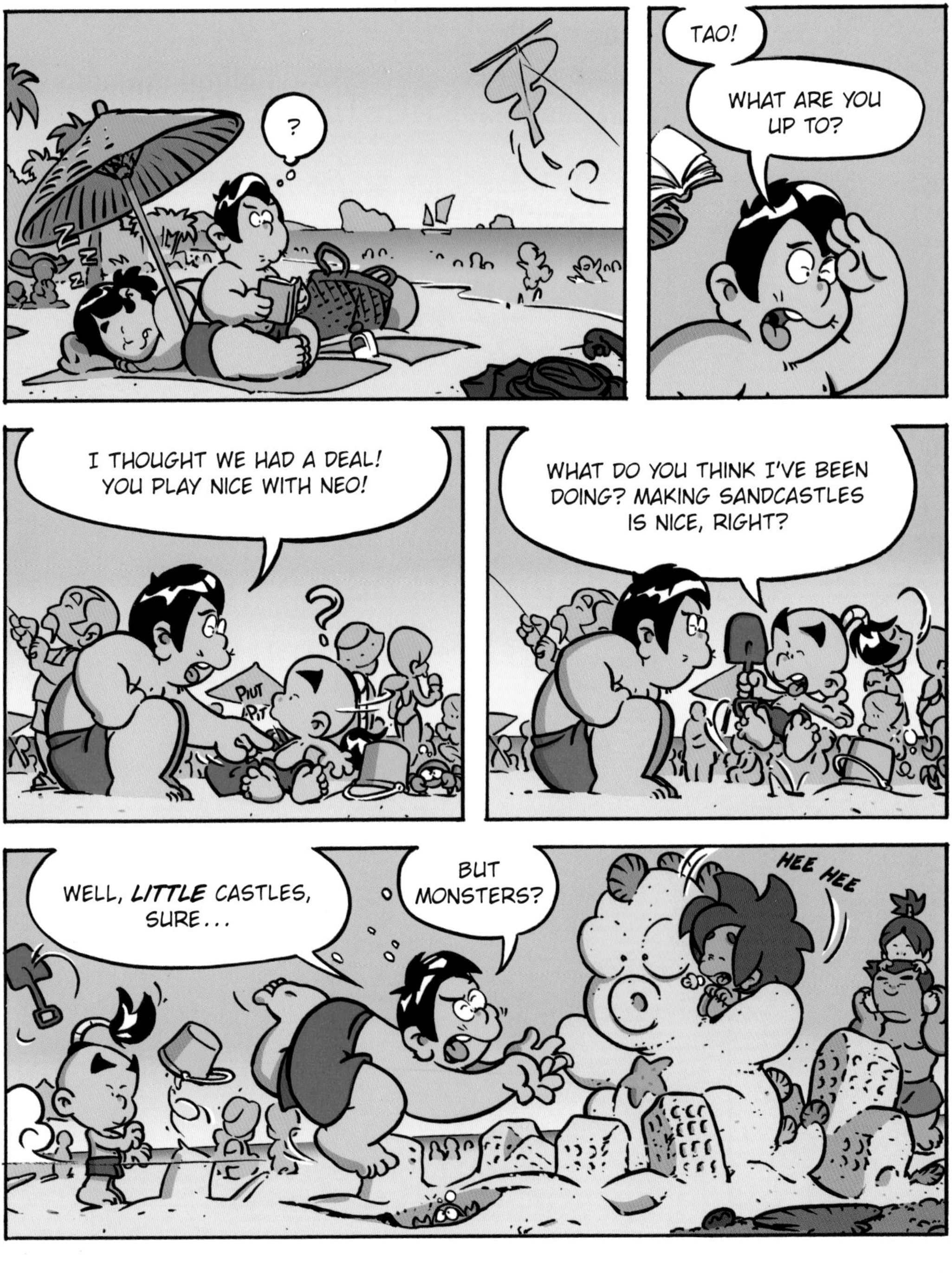
?
TAO!
WHAT ARE YOU UP TO?
I THOUGHT WE HAD A DEAL! YOU PLAY NICE WITH NEO!
PIUT PIT
WHAT DO YOU THINK I'VE BEEN DOING? MAKING SANDCASTLES IS NICE, RIGHT?
WELL, *LITTLE* CASTLES, SURE...
BUT MONSTERS?
HEE HEE

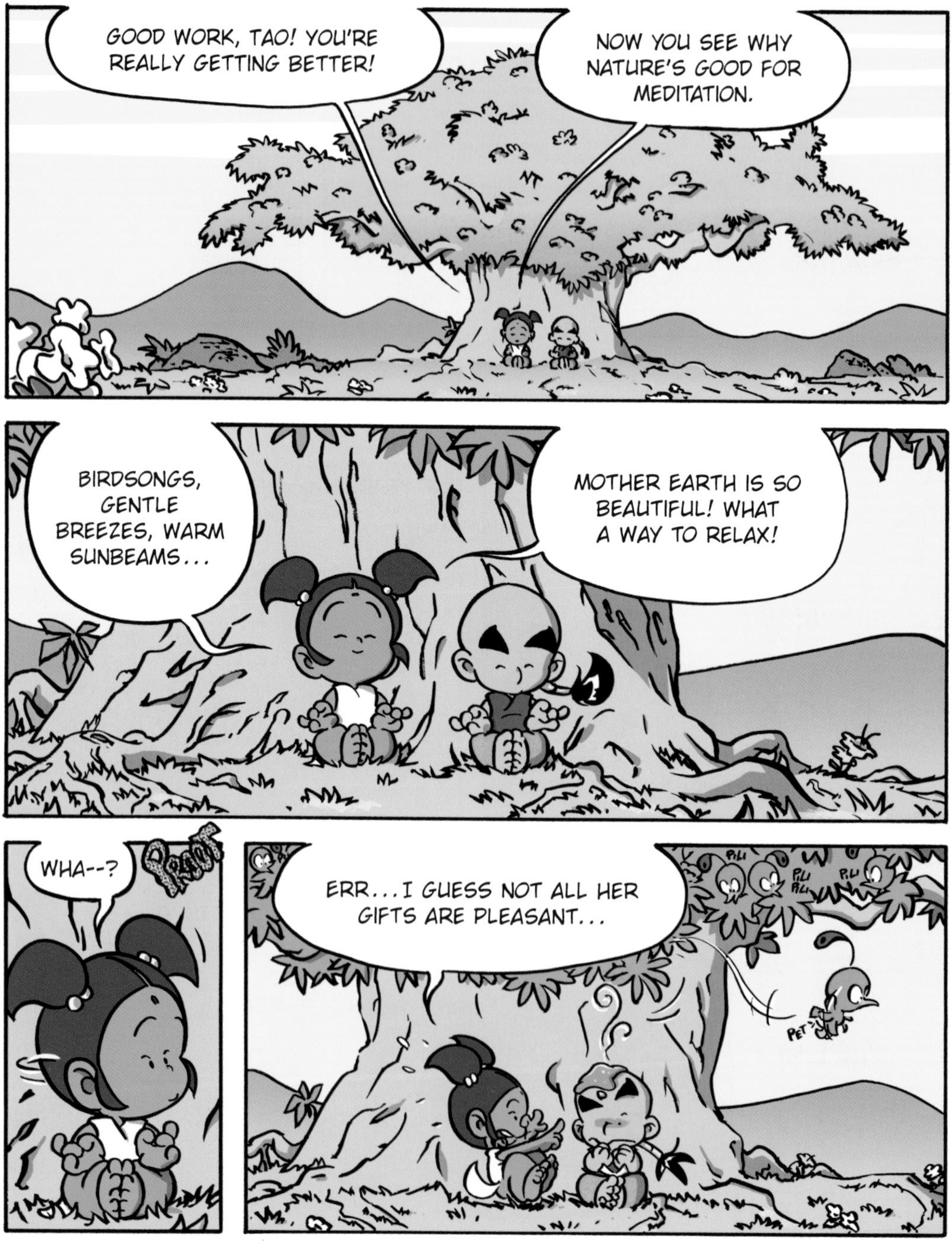
GOOD WORK, TAO! YOU'RE REALLY GETTING BETTER!
NOW YOU SEE WHY NATURE'S GOOD FOR MEDITATION.
BIRDSONGS, GENTLE BREEZES, WARM SUNBEAMS...
MOTHER EARTH IS SO BEAUTIFUL! WHAT A WAY TO RELAX!
WHA--?
PRAAT
PILI
PILI PILI
PILI
ERR...I GUESS NOT ALL HER GIFTS ARE PLEASANT...
PET

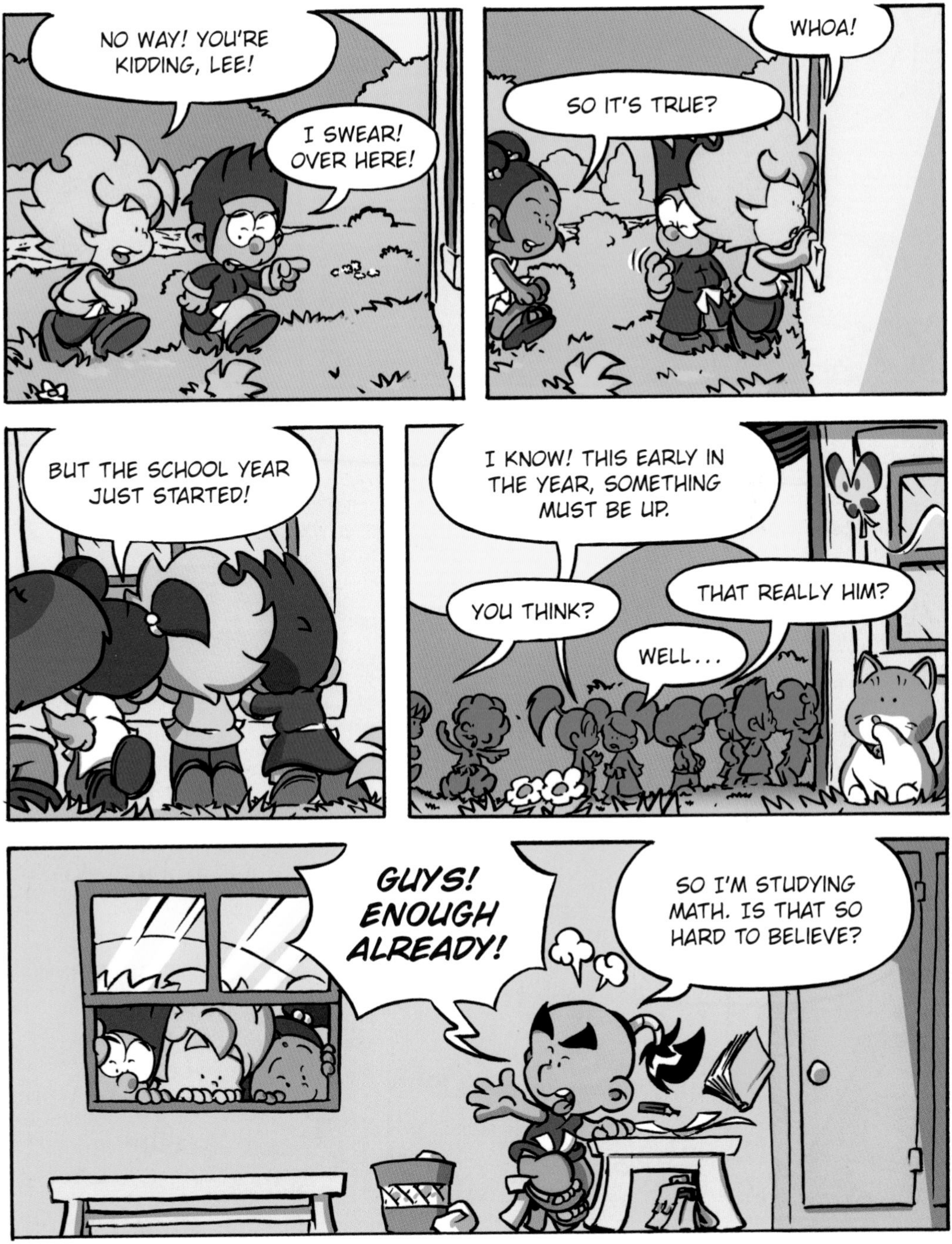
NO WAY! YOU'RE KIDDING, LEE!
I SWEAR! OVER HERE!
WHOA!
SO IT'S TRUE?
BUT THE SCHOOL YEAR JUST STARTED!
I KNOW! THIS EARLY IN THE YEAR, SOMETHING MUST BE UP.
YOU THINK?
THAT REALLY HIM?
WELL...
GUYS! ENOUGH ALREADY!
SO I'M STUDYING MATH. IS THAT SO HARD TO BELIEVE?

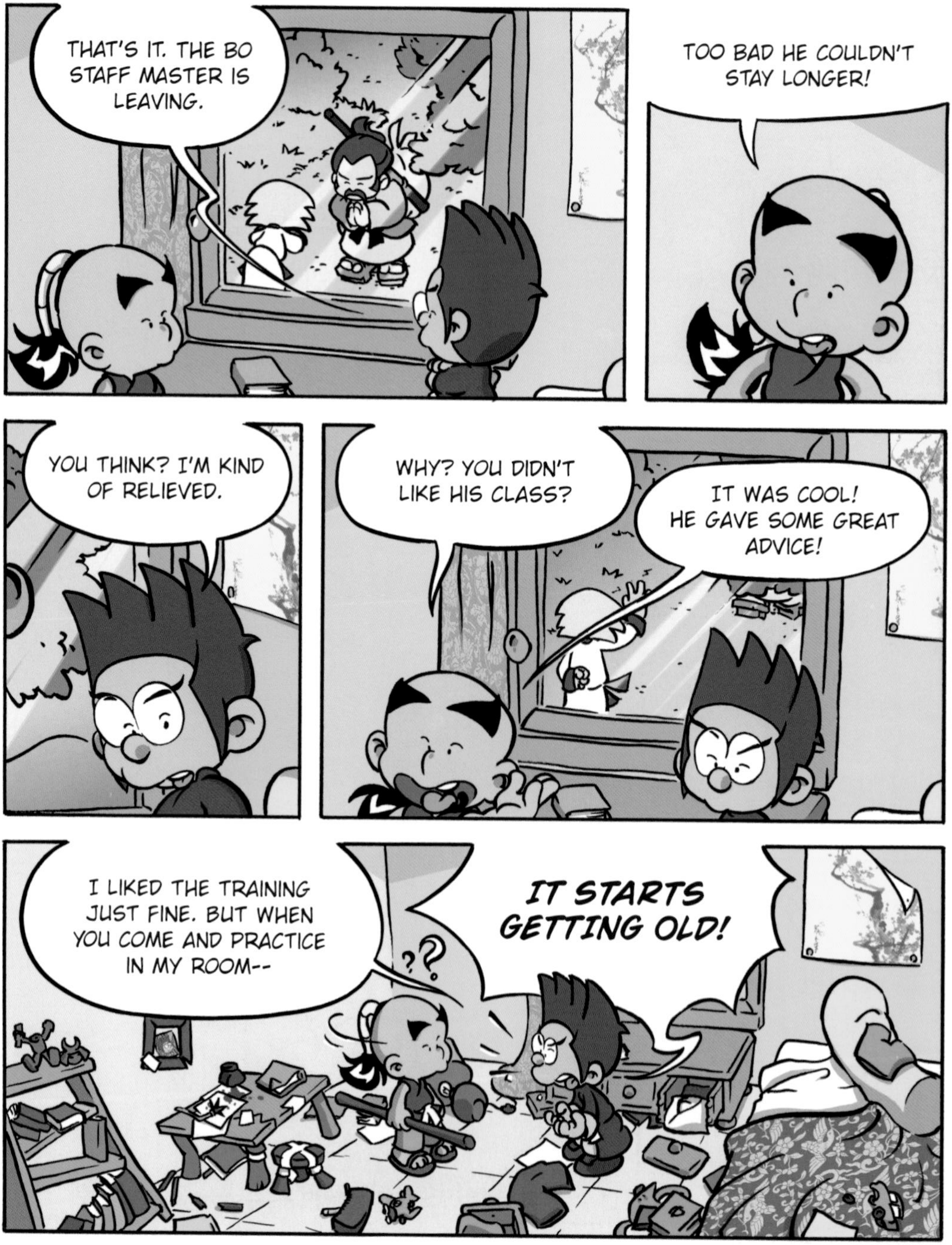
THAT'S IT. THE BO STAFF MASTER IS LEAVING.
TOO BAD HE COULDN'T STAY LONGER!
YOU THINK? I'M KIND OF RELIEVED.
WHY? YOU DIDN'T LIKE HIS CLASS?
IT WAS COOL! HE GAVE SOME GREAT ADVICE!
I LIKED THE TRAINING JUST FINE. BUT WHEN YOU COME AND PRACTICE IN MY ROOM--
??
IT STARTS GETTING OLD!

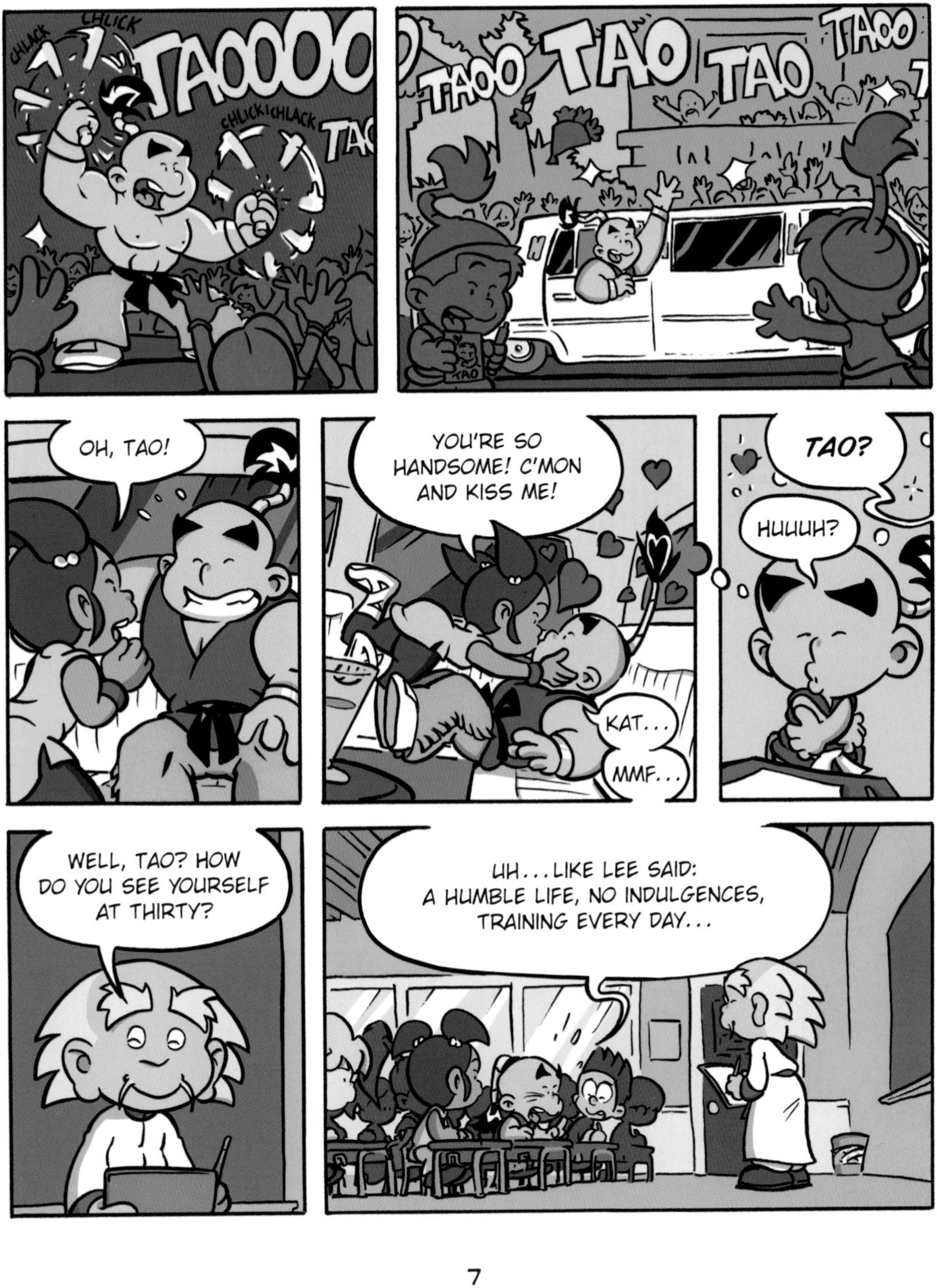
CHLACK
CHLICK
TAOOOO
CHLICK! CHLACK
TAO
TAOO TAO TAO TAOO
TAO
OH, TAO!
YOU'RE SO HANDSOME! C'MON AND KISS ME!
KAT...
MMF...
TAO?
HUUUH?
WELL, TAO? HOW DO YOU SEE YOURSELF AT THIRTY?
UH...LIKE LEE SAID: A HUMBLE LIFE, NO INDULGENCES, TRAINING EVERY DAY...

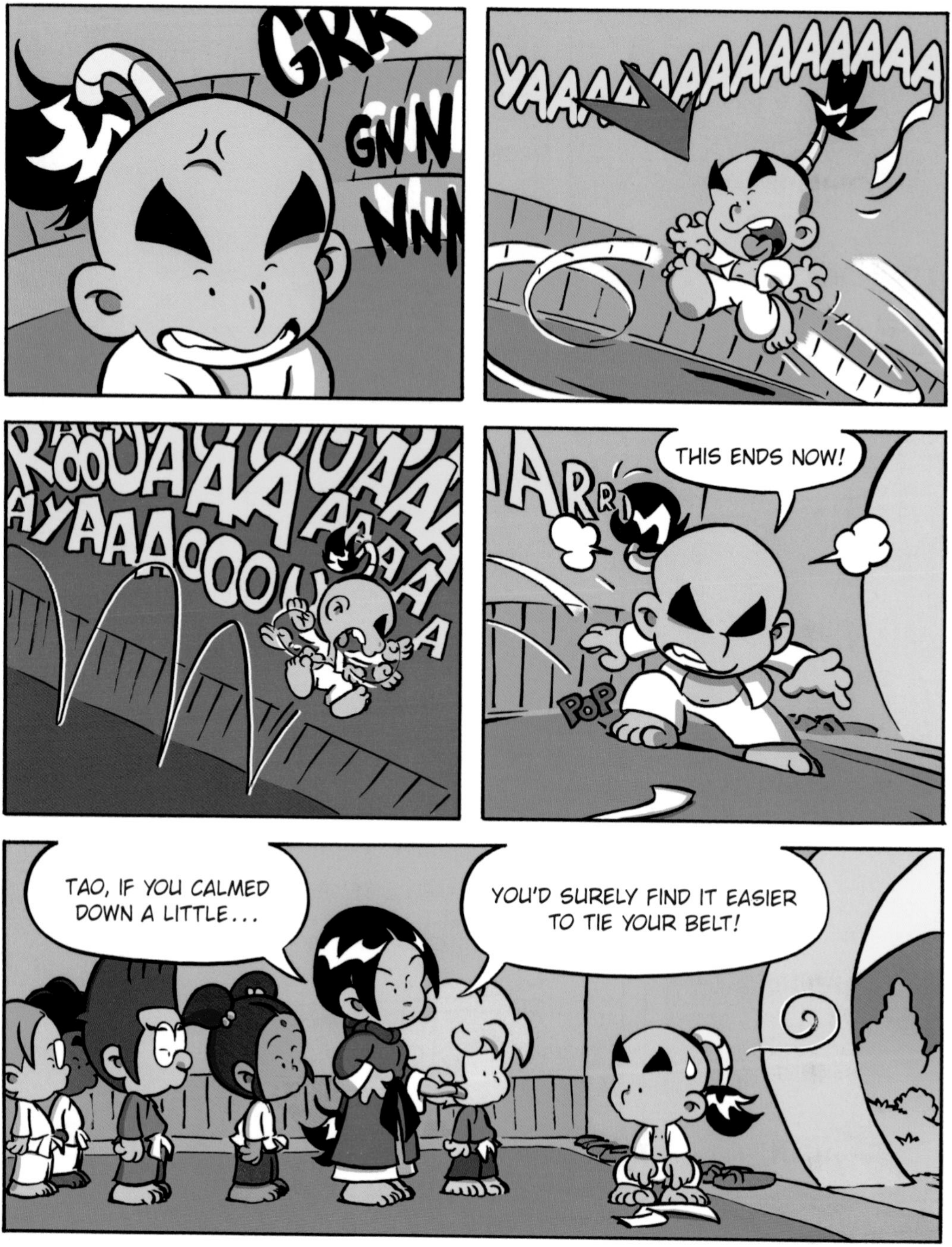
GNN
THIS ENDS NOW!
ARR
POP
TAO, IF YOU CALMED DOWN A LITTLE...
YOU'D SURELY FIND IT EASIER TO TIE YOUR BELT!

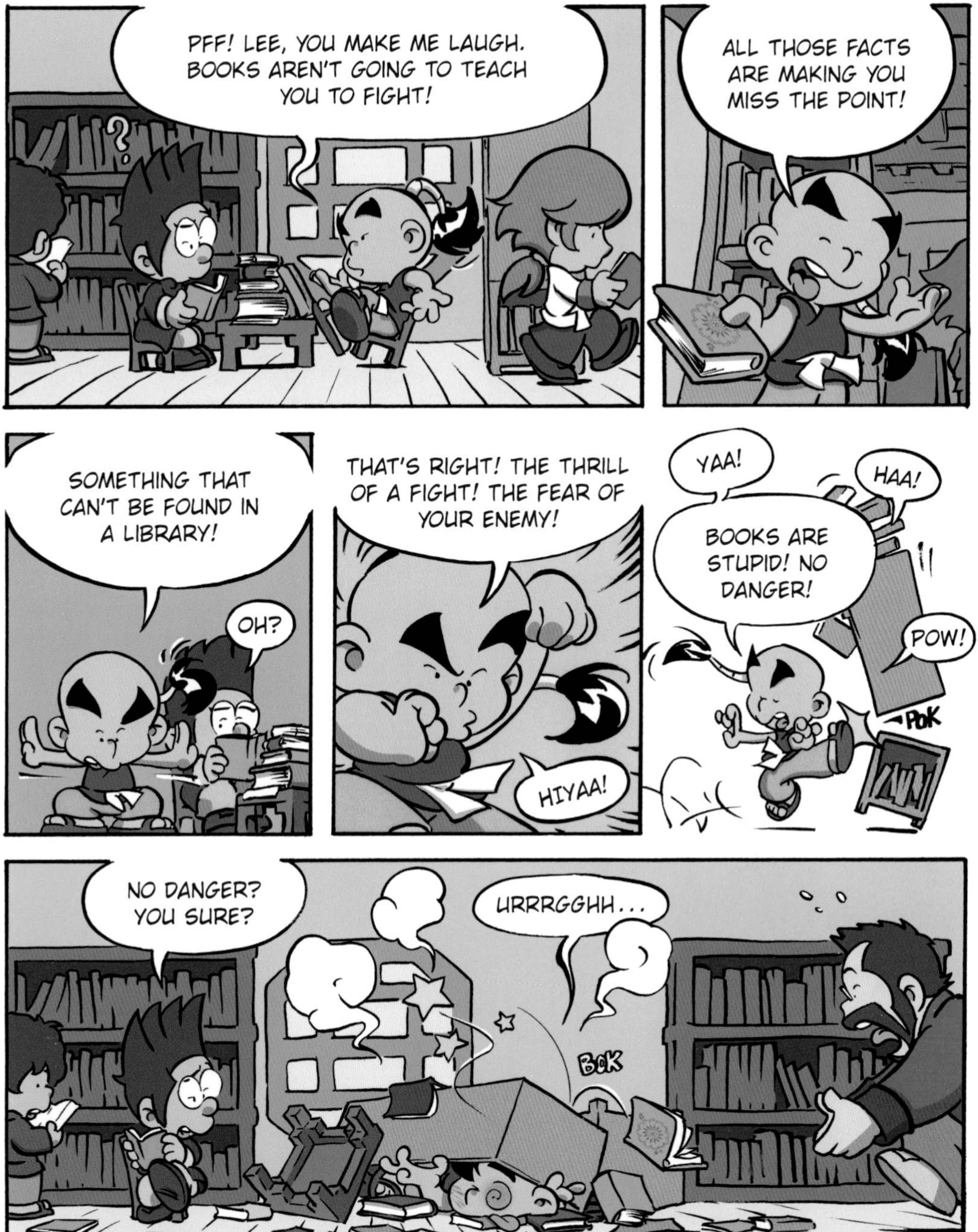
PFF! LEE, YOU MAKE ME LAUGH. BOOKS AREN'T GOING TO TEACH YOU TO FIGHT!
?
ALL THOSE FACTS ARE MAKING YOU MISS THE POINT!
SOMETHING THAT CAN'T BE FOUND IN A LIBRARY!
OH?
THAT'S RIGHT! THE THRILL OF A FIGHT! THE FEAR OF YOUR ENEMY!
HIYAA!
YAA!
HAA!
BOOKS ARE STUPID! NO DANGER!
POW!
POK
NO DANGER? YOU SURE?
URRRGGHH...
BOK

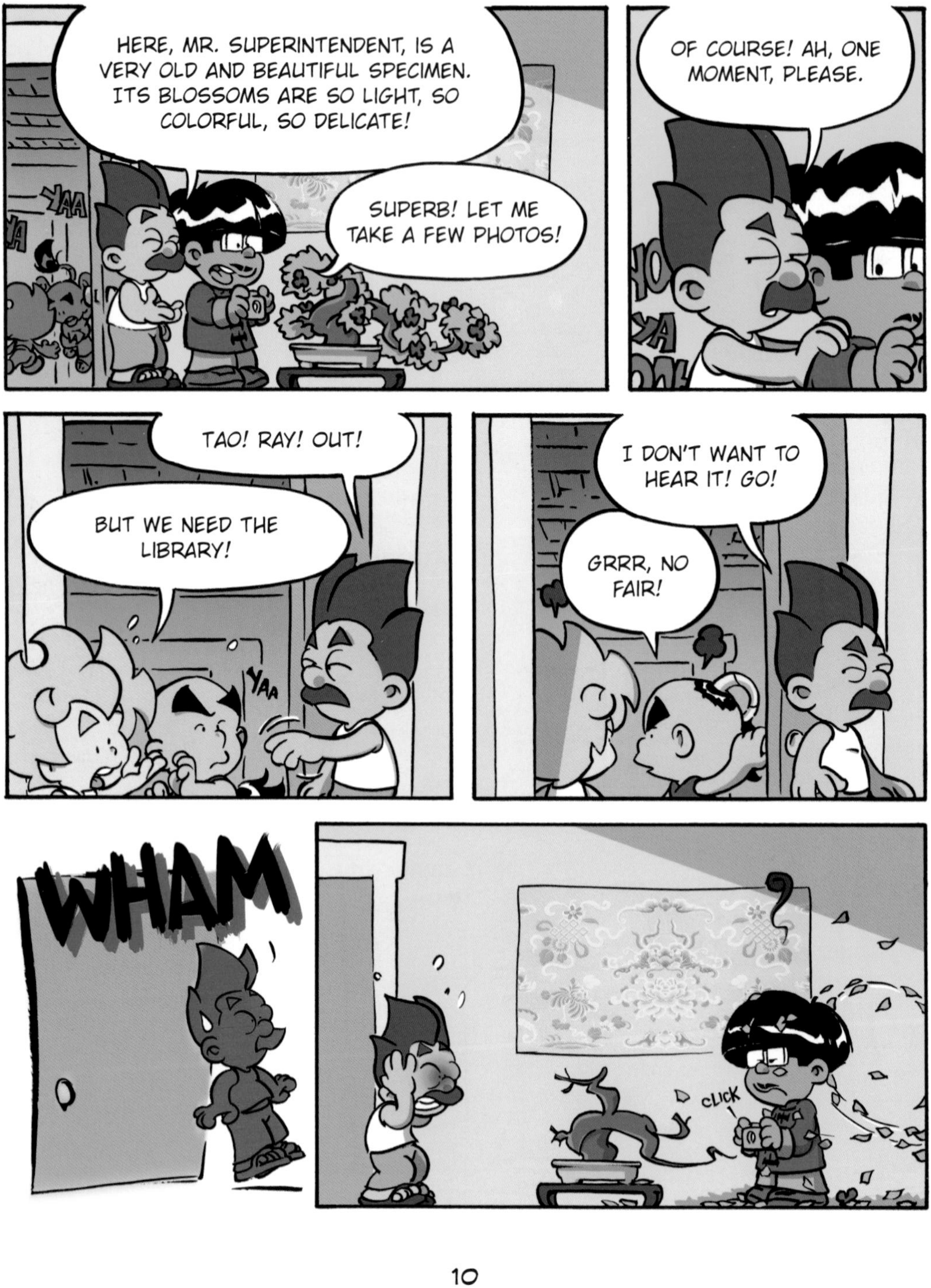
HERE, MR. SUPERINTENDENT, IS A VERY OLD AND BEAUTIFUL SPECIMEN. ITS BLOSSOMS ARE SO LIGHT, SO COLORFUL, SO DELICATE!
SUPERB! LET ME TAKE A FEW PHOTOS!
OF COURSE! AH, ONE MOMENT, PLEASE.
TAO! RAY! OUT!
BUT WE NEED THE LIBRARY!
YAA
I DON'T WANT TO HEAR IT! GO!
GRRR, NO FAIR!
WHAM
CLICK

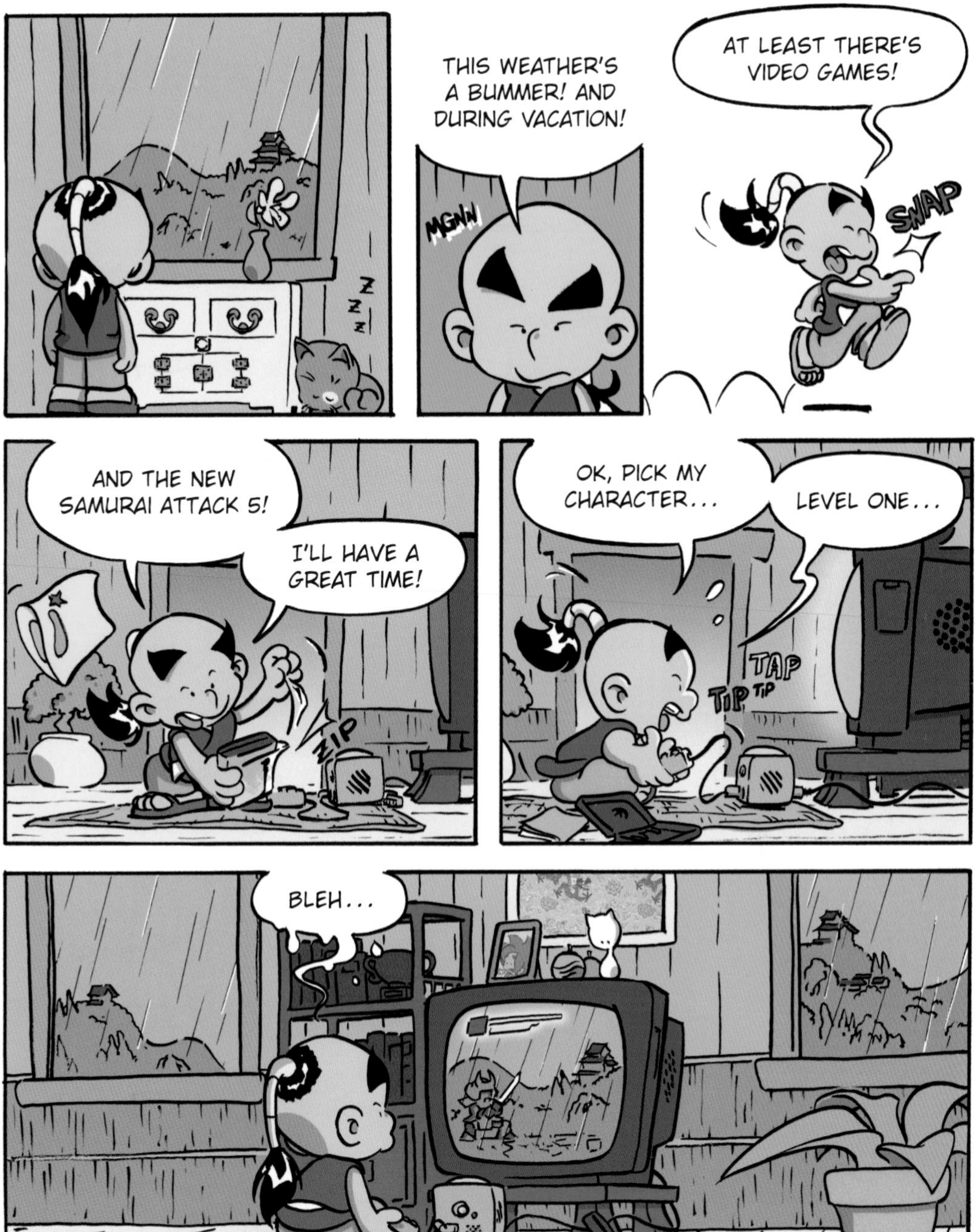
THIS WEATHER'S A BUMMER! AND DURING VACATION!
MGNN
AT LEAST THERE'S VIDEO GAMES!
SNAP
AND THE NEW SAMURAI ATTACK 5!
I'LL HAVE A GREAT TIME!
ZIP
OK, PICK MY CHARACTER...
LEVEL ONE...
TAP
TIP TIP
BLEH...

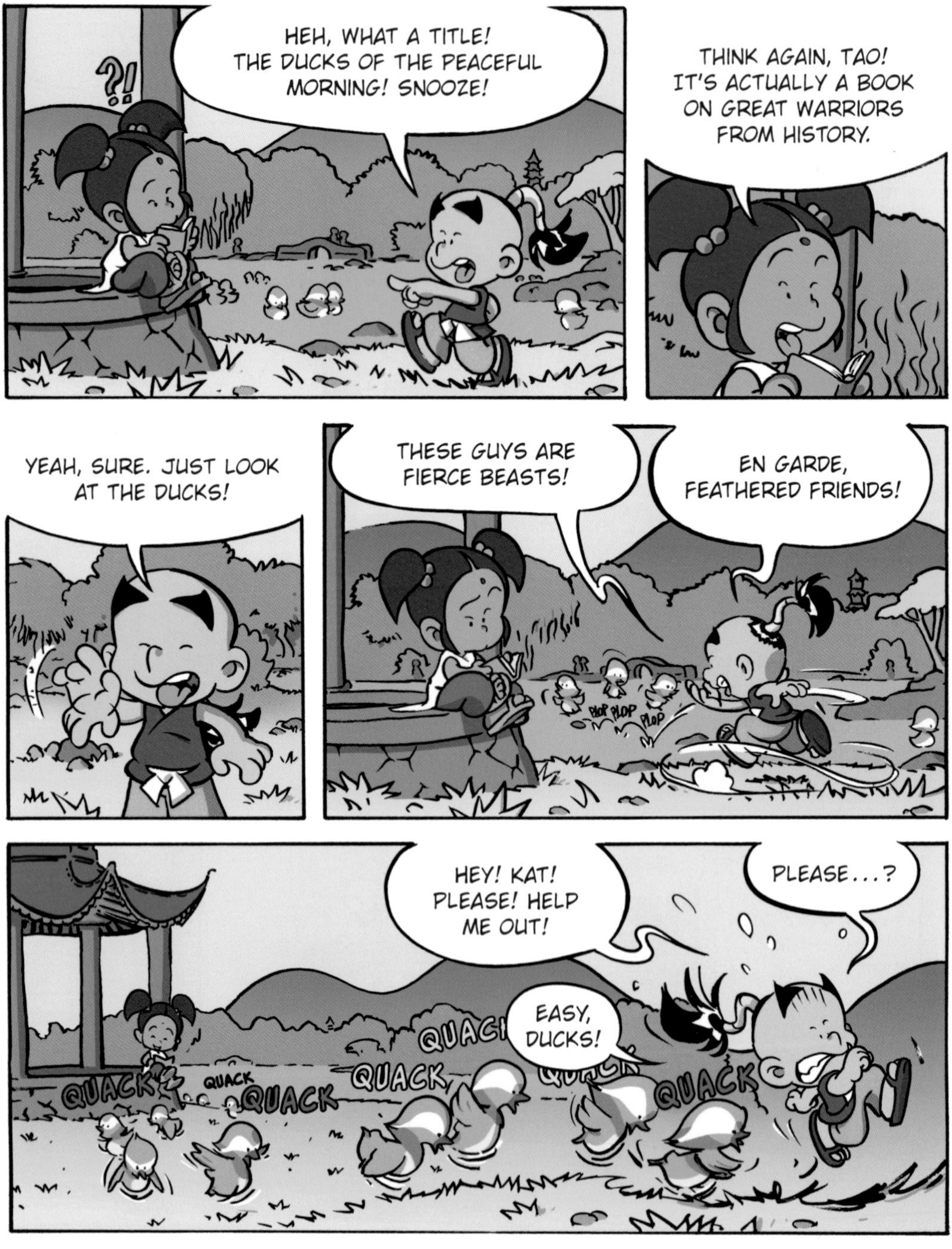
?!
HEH, WHAT A TITLE! THE DUCKS OF THE PEACEFUL MORNING! SNOOZE!
THINK AGAIN, TAO! IT'S ACTUALLY A BOOK ON GREAT WARRIORS FROM HISTORY.
YEAH, SURE. JUST LOOK AT THE DUCKS!
THESE GUYS ARE FIERCE BEASTS!
EN GARDE, FEATHERED FRIENDS!
PLOP PLOP PLOP
HEY! KAT! PLEASE! HELP ME OUT!
PLEASE...?
EASY, DUCKS!
QUACK QUACK QUACK QUACK QUACK QUACK

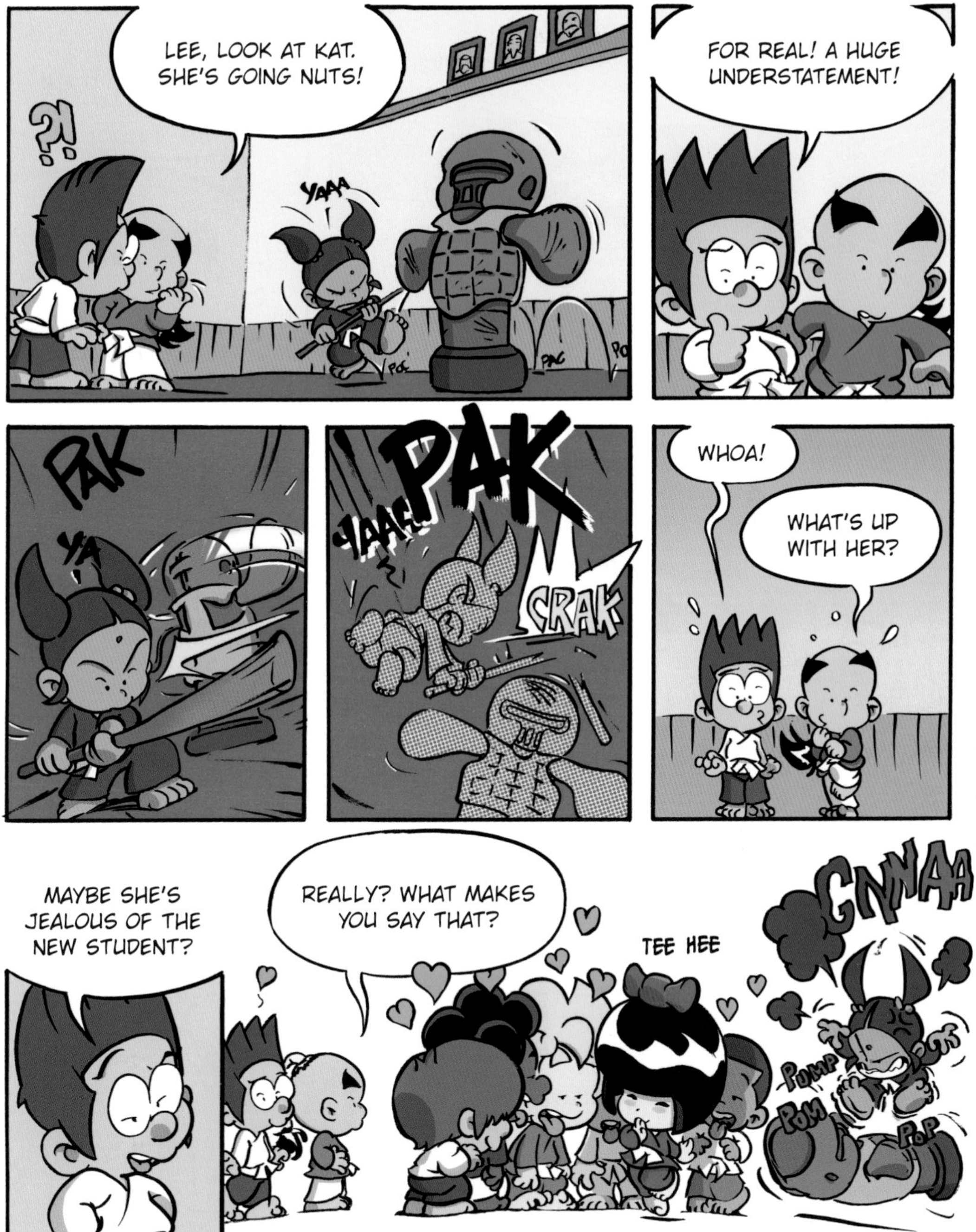

?!
LEE, LOOK AT KAT. SHE'S GOING NUTS!
YAAA
FOR REAL! A HUGE UNDERSTATEMENT!
PAK
YA
PAK
CRAK
WHOA!
WHAT'S UP WITH HER?
MAYBE SHE'S JEALOUS OF THE NEW STUDENT?
REALLY? WHAT MAKES YOU SAY THAT?
TEE HEE
GNNAA
POMP
POM

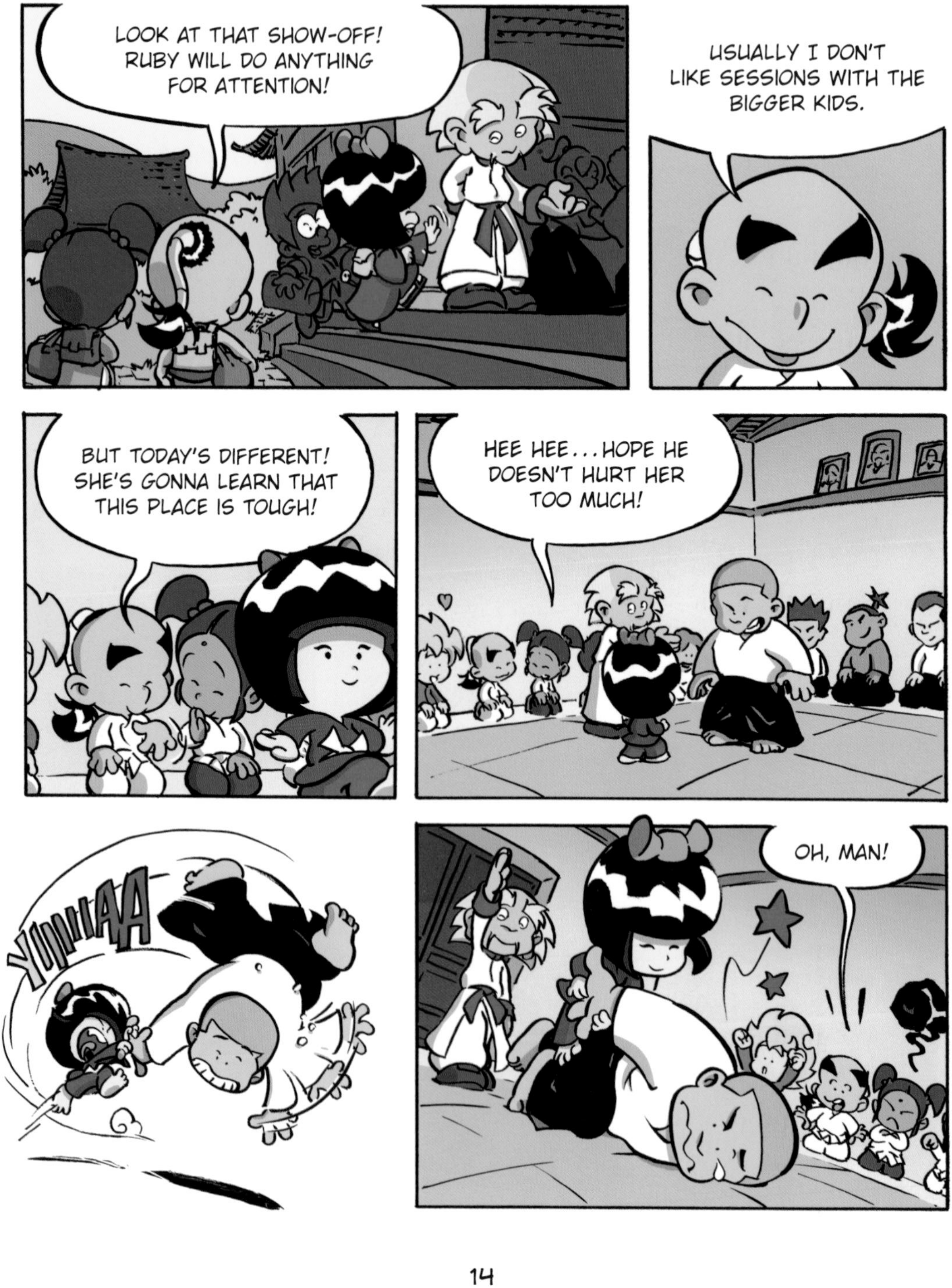
LOOK AT THAT SHOW-OFF! RUBY WILL DO ANYTHING FOR ATTENTION!
USUALLY I DON'T LIKE SESSIONS WITH THE BIGGER KIDS.
BUT TODAY'S DIFFERENT! SHE'S GONNA LEARN THAT THIS PLACE IS TOUGH!
HEE HEE...HOPE HE DOESN'T HURT HER TOO MUCH!
YIIIIIAA
OH, MAN!

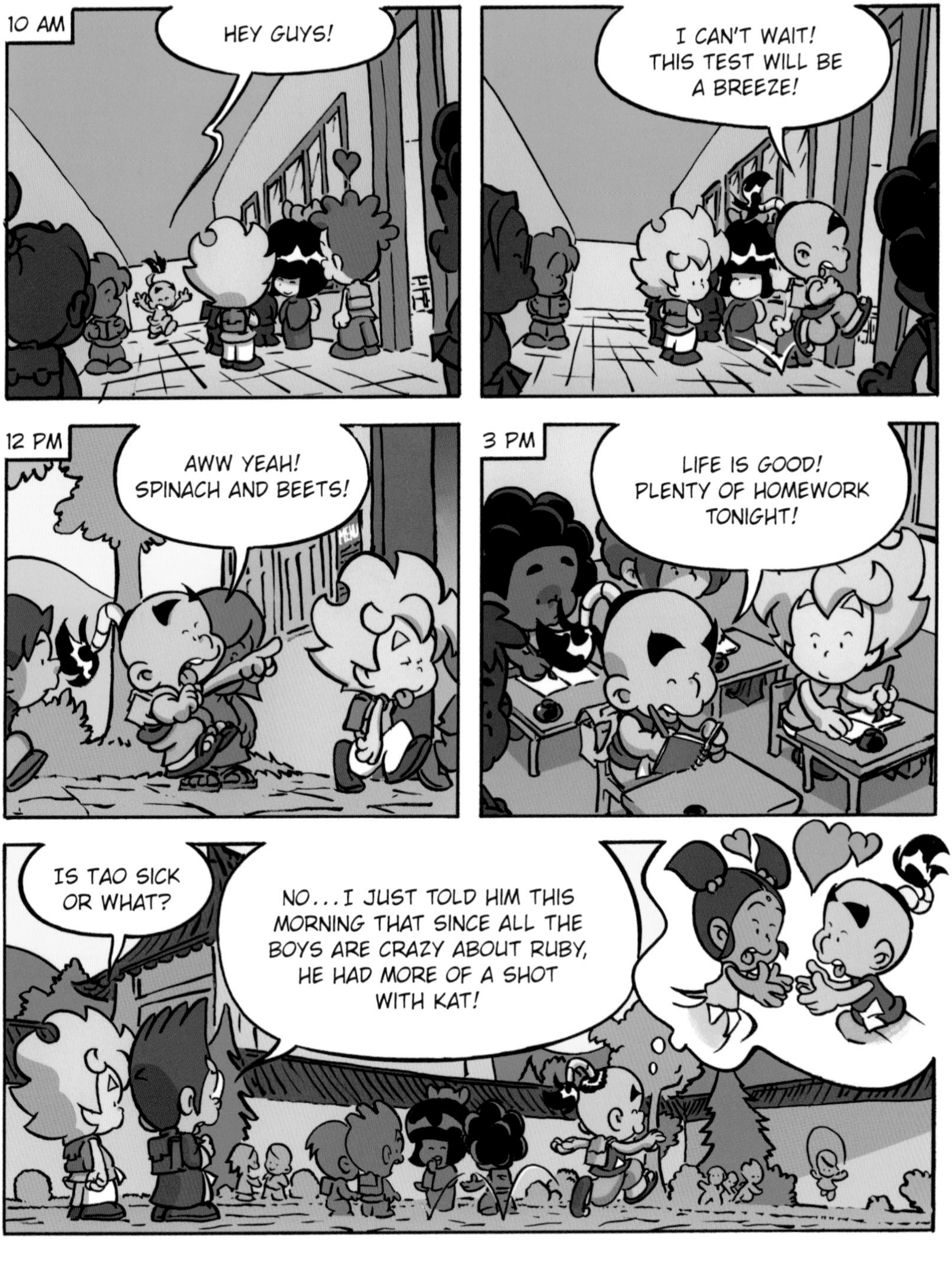
10 AM
HEY GUYS!
I CAN'T WAIT! THIS TEST WILL BE A BREEZE!
12 PM
AWW YEAH! SPINACH AND BEETS!
3 PM
LIFE IS GOOD! PLENTY OF HOMEWORK TONIGHT!
IS TAO SICK OR WHAT?
NO...I JUST TOLD HIM THIS MORNING THAT SINCE ALL THE BOYS ARE CRAZY ABOUT RUBY, HE HAD MORE OF A SHOT WITH KAT!

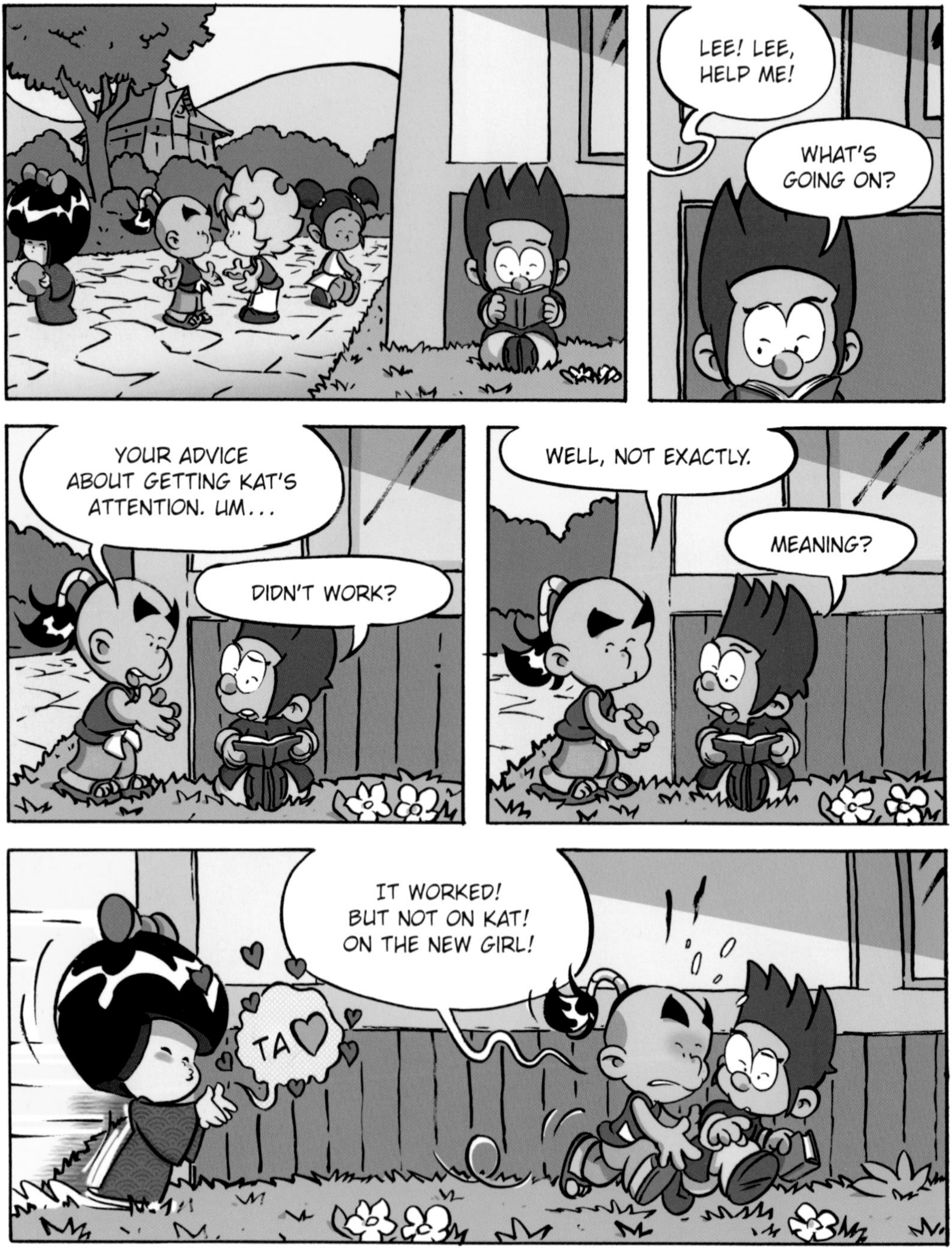

LEE! LEE, HELP ME!
WHAT'S GOING ON?
YOUR ADVICE ABOUT GETTING KAT'S ATTENTION. UM...
DIDN'T WORK?
WELL, NOT EXACTLY.
MEANING?
IT WORKED! BUT NOT ON KAT! ON THE NEW GIRL!
TA

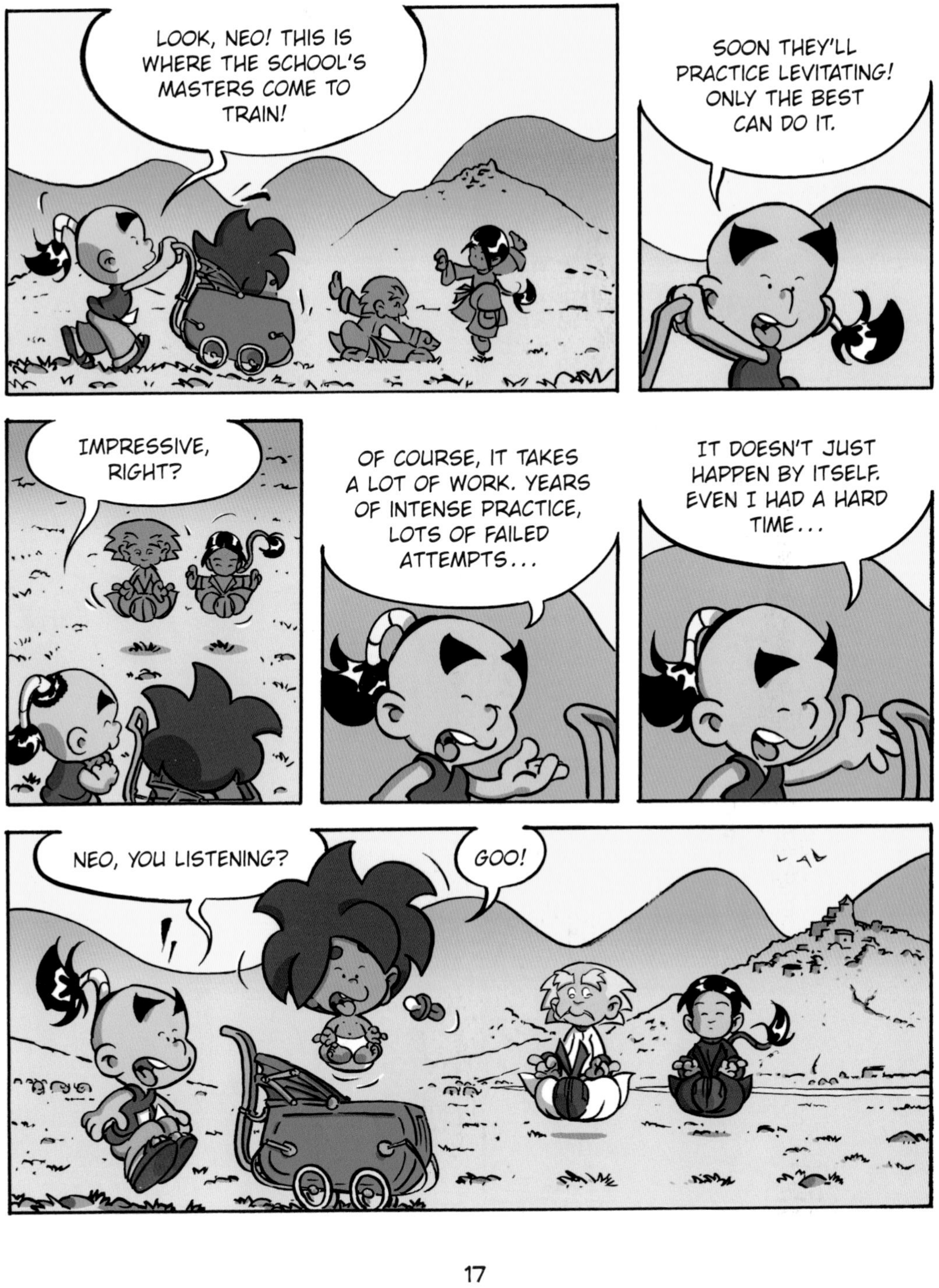
LOOK, NEO! THIS IS WHERE THE SCHOOL'S MASTERS COME TO TRAIN!
SOON THEY'LL PRACTICE LEVITATING! ONLY THE BEST CAN DO IT.
IMPRESSIVE, RIGHT?
OF COURSE, IT TAKES A LOT OF WORK. YEARS OF INTENSE PRACTICE, LOTS OF FAILED ATTEMPTS...
IT DOESN'T JUST HAPPEN BY ITSELF. EVEN I HAD A HARD TIME...
NEO, YOU LISTENING?
GOO!

WHAT'S THE MATTER, KAT?

SNIFF

DON'T TELL ME IT'S STILL THAT NEW GIRL?

SERIOUSLY, NO NEED TO BE JEALOUS OF RUBY. YOU'RE THE BEST AT JUDO!

OOOAAAOOUUUUIIII

HUH?

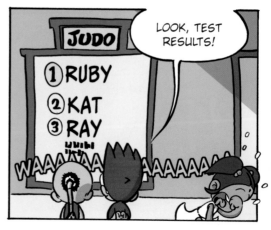

LOOK, TEST RESULTS!

JUDO

1 RUBY

2 KAT

3 RAY

WAAAAAAAAAAAAAAA

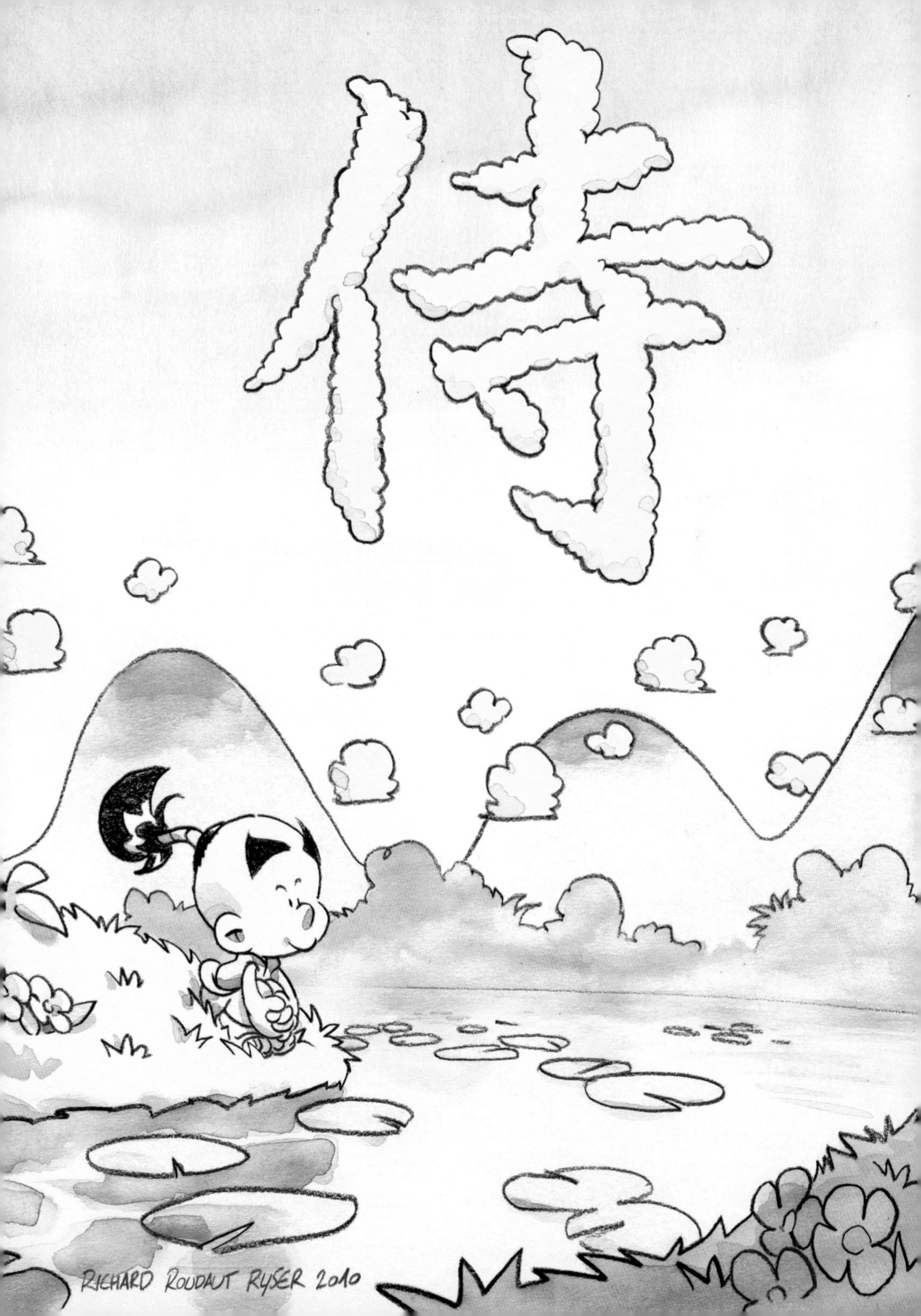
侍
RICHARD ROUDAUT RYSER 2010

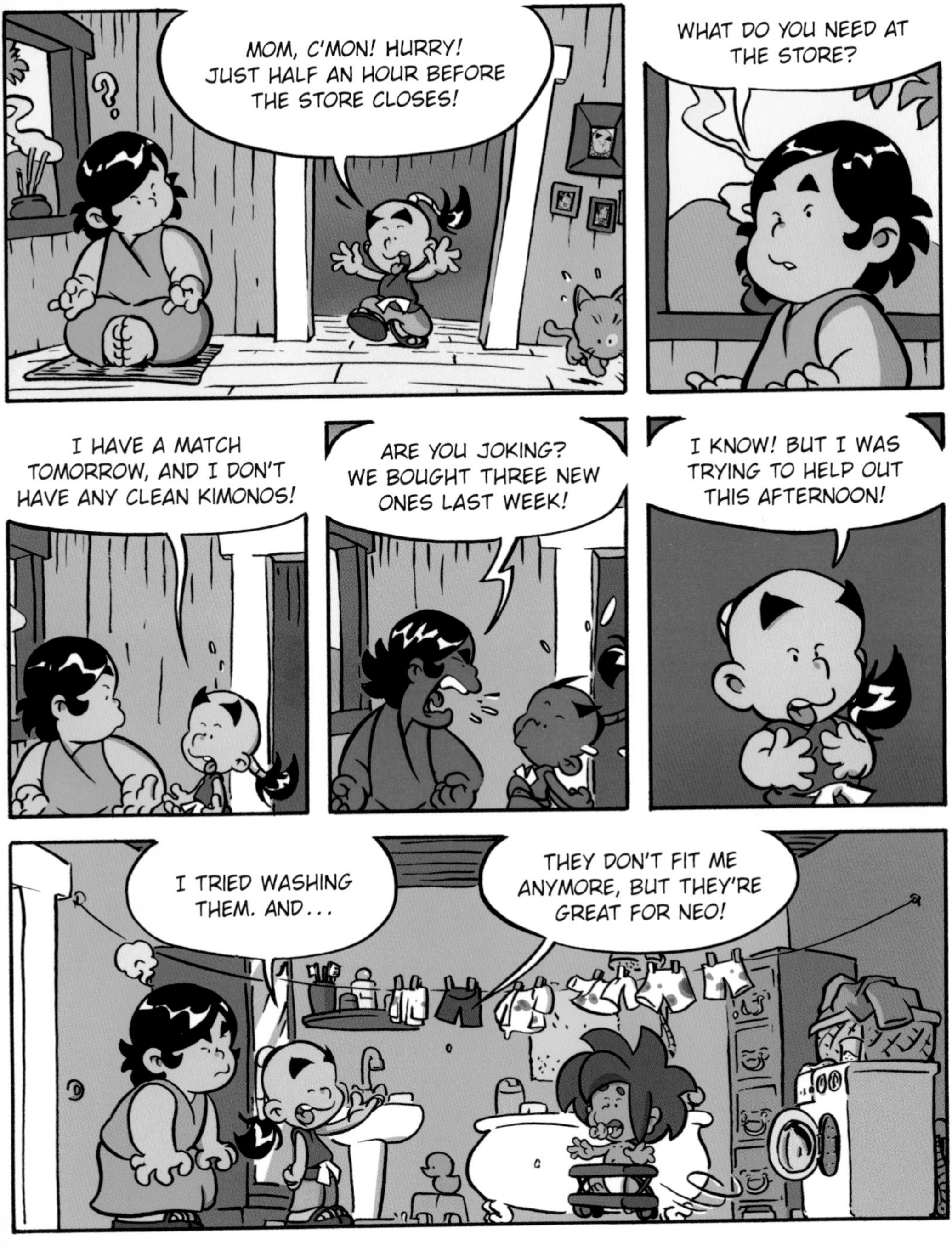
MOM, C'MON! HURRY! JUST HALF AN HOUR BEFORE THE STORE CLOSES!
WHAT DO YOU NEED AT THE STORE?
I HAVE A MATCH TOMORROW, AND I DON'T HAVE ANY CLEAN KIMONOS!
ARE YOU JOKING? WE BOUGHT THREE NEW ONES LAST WEEK!
I KNOW! BUT I WAS TRYING TO HELP OUT THIS AFTERNOON!
I TRIED WASHING THEM. AND...
THEY DON'T FIT ME ANYMORE, BUT THEY'RE GREAT FOR NEO!

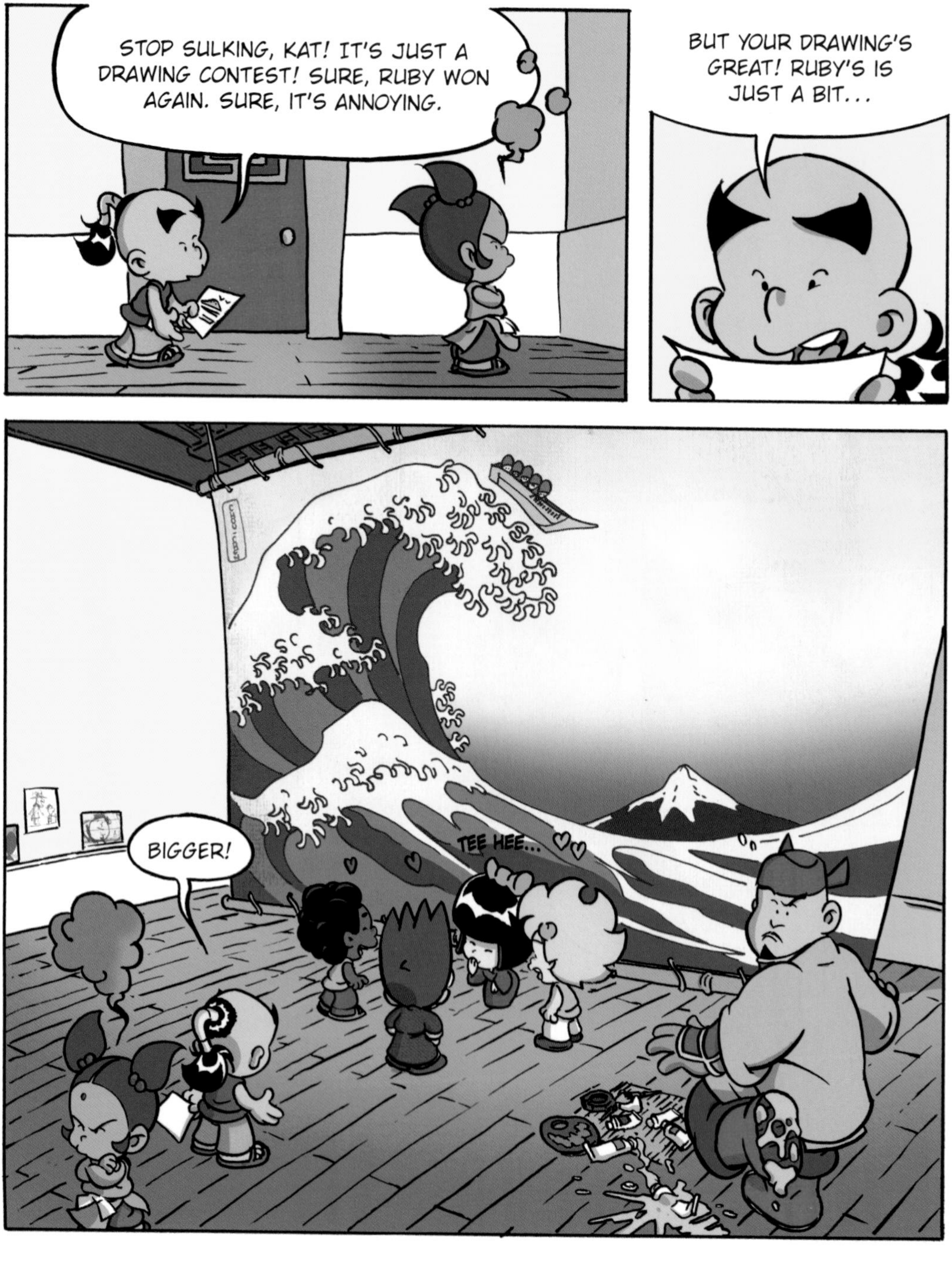
STOP SULKING, KAT! IT'S JUST A DRAWING CONTEST! SURE, RUBY WON AGAIN. SURE, IT'S ANNOYING.
BUT YOUR DRAWING'S GREAT! RUBY'S IS JUST A BIT...
BIGGER!
TEE HEE...

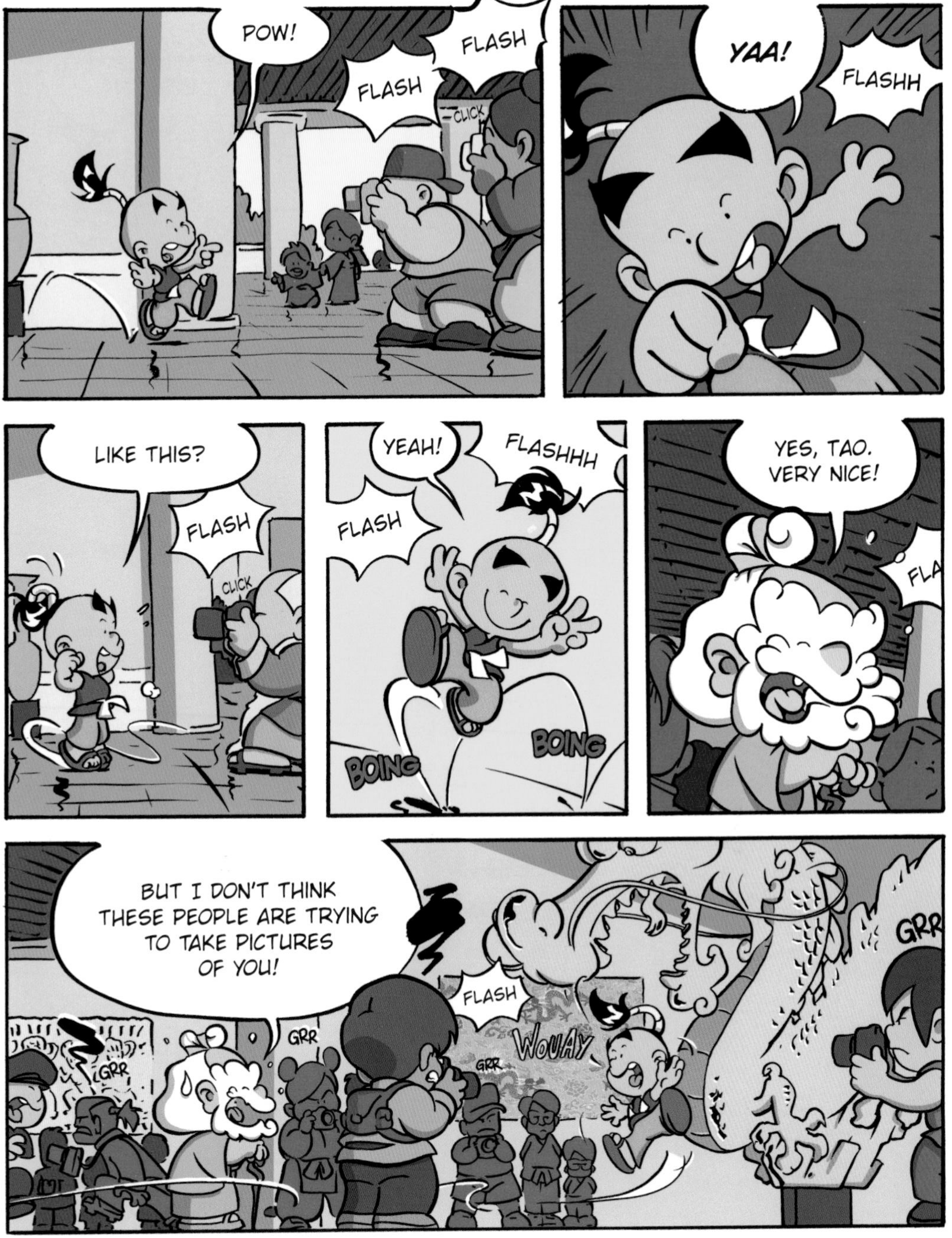
POW!
FLASH
FLASH
CLICK
YAA!
FLASHH
LIKE THIS?
FLASH
CLICK
YEAH!
FLASHHH
FLASH
BOING
BOING
YES, TAO. VERY NICE!
BUT I DON'T THINK THESE PEOPLE ARE TRYING TO TAKE PICTURES OF YOU!
FLASH
WOUAY
GRR
GRR
GRR
GRR

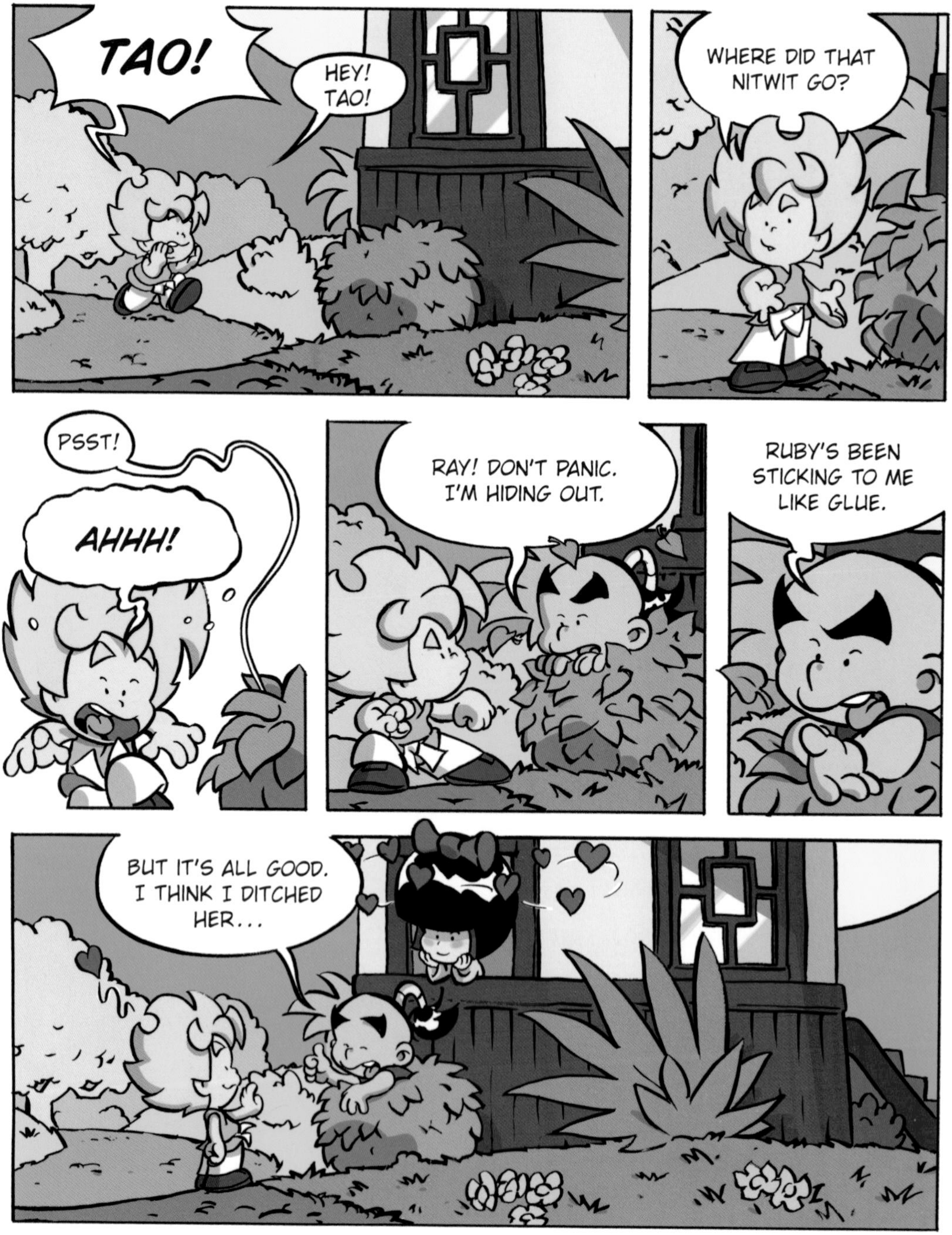

TAO!
HEY! TAO!
WHERE DID THAT NITWIT GO?
PSST!
AHHH!
RAY! DON'T PANIC. I'M HIDING OUT.
RUBY'S BEEN STICKING TO ME LIKE GLUE.
BUT IT'S ALL GOOD. I THINK I DITCHED HER...

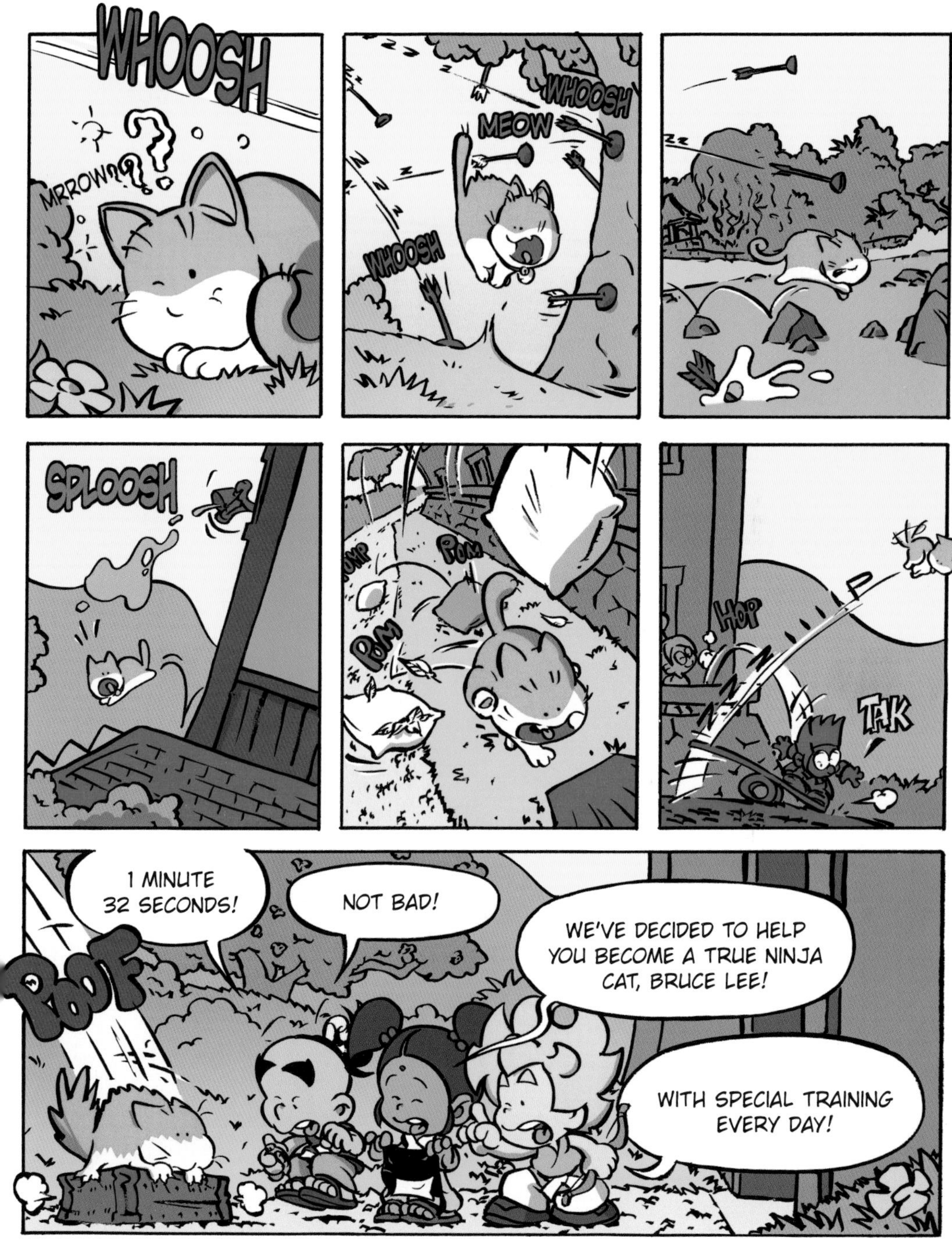
WHOOSH
MRROW??
WHOOSH
MEOW
WHOOSH
SPLOOSH
POM
POM
?!
HOP
TAK
POOF
1 MINUTE 32 SECONDS!
NOT BAD!
WE'VE DECIDED TO HELP YOU BECOME A TRUE NINJA CAT, BRUCE LEE!
WITH SPECIAL TRAINING EVERY DAY!

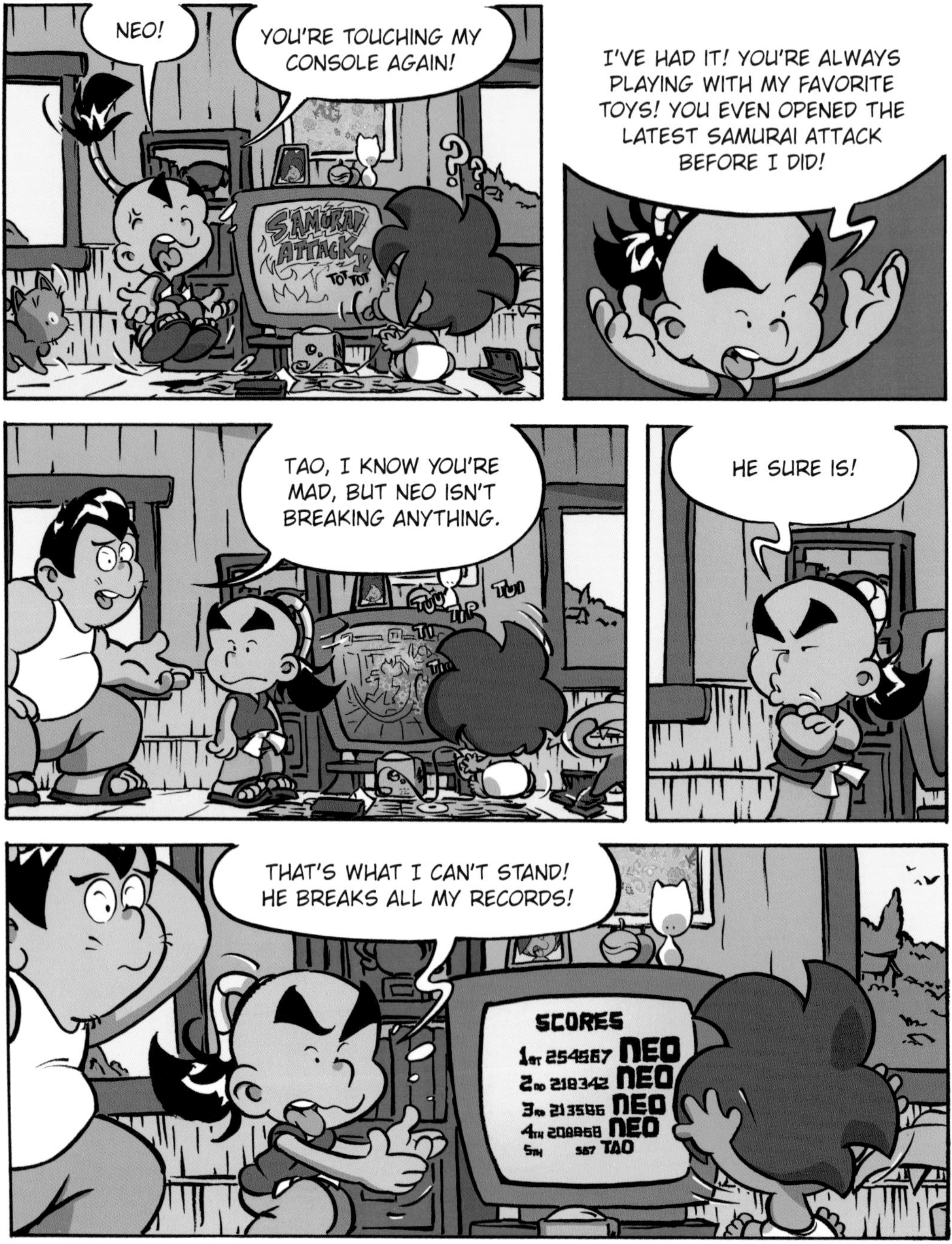
NEO!
YOU'RE TOUCHING MY CONSOLE AGAIN!
SAMURAI ATTACK
TOT TOT
I'VE HAD IT! YOU'RE ALWAYS PLAYING WITH MY FAVORITE TOYS! YOU EVEN OPENED THE LATEST SAMURAI ATTACK BEFORE I DID!
TAO, I KNOW YOU'RE MAD, BUT NEO ISN'T BREAKING ANYTHING.
HE SURE IS!
THAT'S WHAT I CAN'T STAND! HE BREAKS ALL MY RECORDS!
SCORES
1ST 254567 NEO
2ND 218342 NEO
3RD 213586 NEO
4TH 208868 NEO
5TH 587 TAO

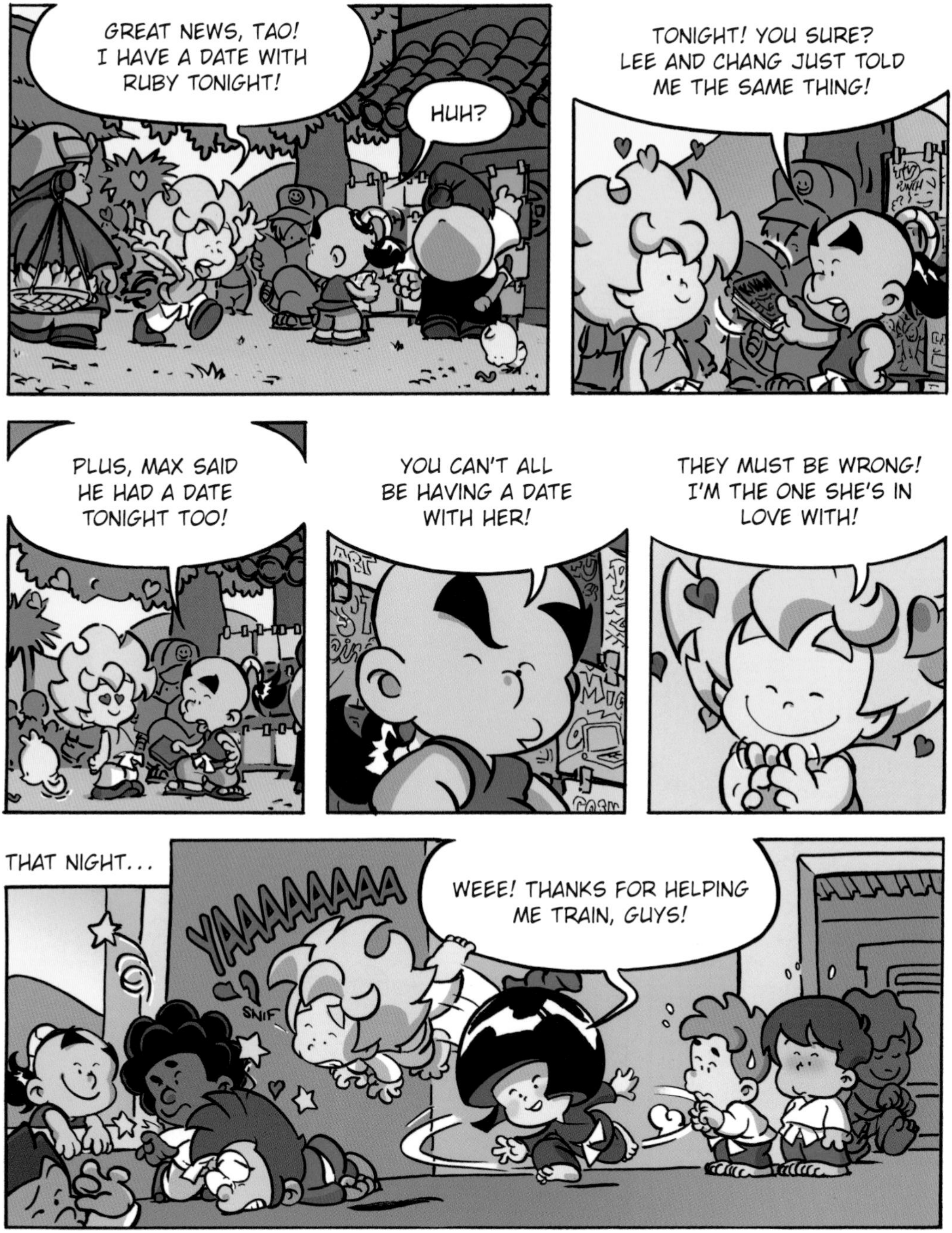
GREAT NEWS, TAO! I HAVE A DATE WITH RUBY TONIGHT!
HUH?
TONIGHT! YOU SURE? LEE AND CHANG JUST TOLD ME THE SAME THING!
PLUS, MAX SAID HE HAD A DATE TONIGHT TOO!
YOU CAN'T ALL BE HAVING A DATE WITH HER!
THEY MUST BE WRONG! I'M THE ONE SHE'S IN LOVE WITH!
THAT NIGHT...
YAAAAAAAA
WEEE! THANKS FOR HELPING ME TRAIN, GUYS!
SNIF

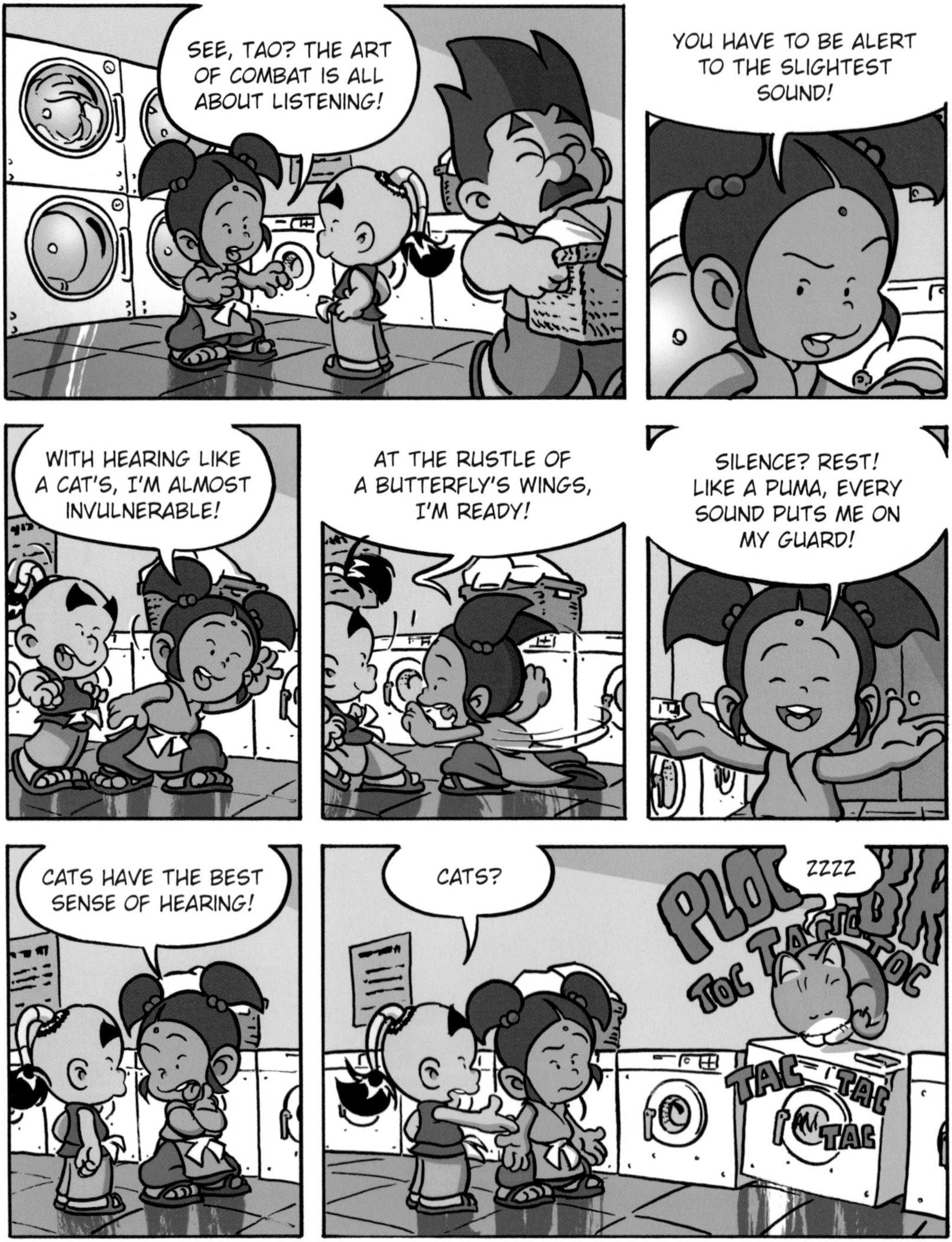
SEE, TAO? THE ART OF COMBAT IS ALL ABOUT LISTENING!
YOU HAVE TO BE ALERT TO THE SLIGHTEST SOUND!
WITH HEARING LIKE A CAT'S, I'M ALMOST INVULNERABLE!
AT THE RUSTLE OF A BUTTERFLY'S WINGS, I'M READY!
SILENCE? REST! LIKE A PUMA, EVERY SOUND PUTS ME ON MY GUARD!
CATS HAVE THE BEST SENSE OF HEARING!
CATS?
ZZZZ
TOC TAC TOC TOC
TAC TAC TAC

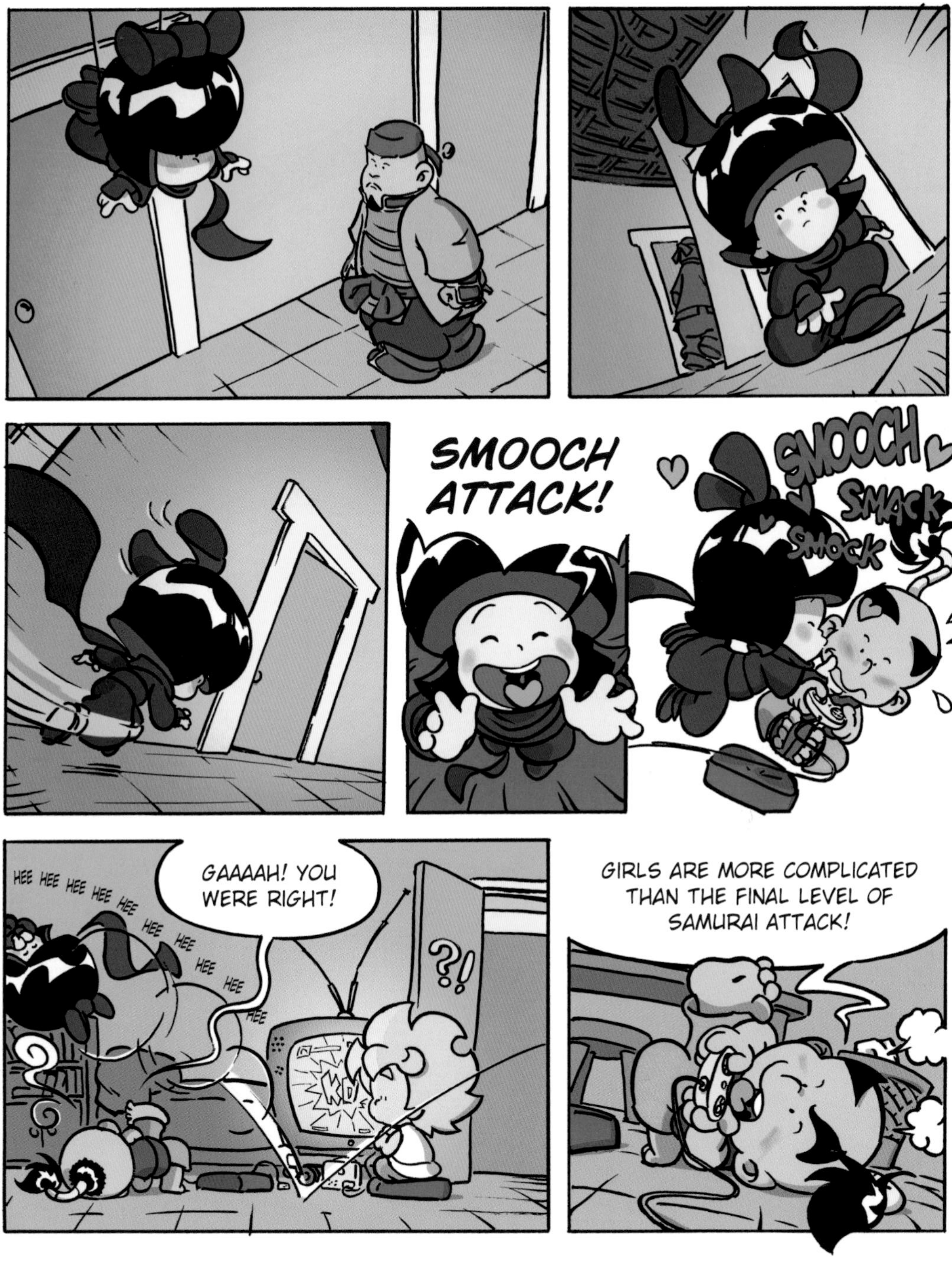
SMOOCH ATTACK!
SMOOCH
SMACK
SMOCK
HEE HEE HEE HEE HEE HEE HEE HEE HEE HEE
GAAAAH! YOU WERE RIGHT!
?!
KO
GIRLS ARE MORE COMPLICATED THAN THE FINAL LEVEL OF SAMURAI ATTACK!

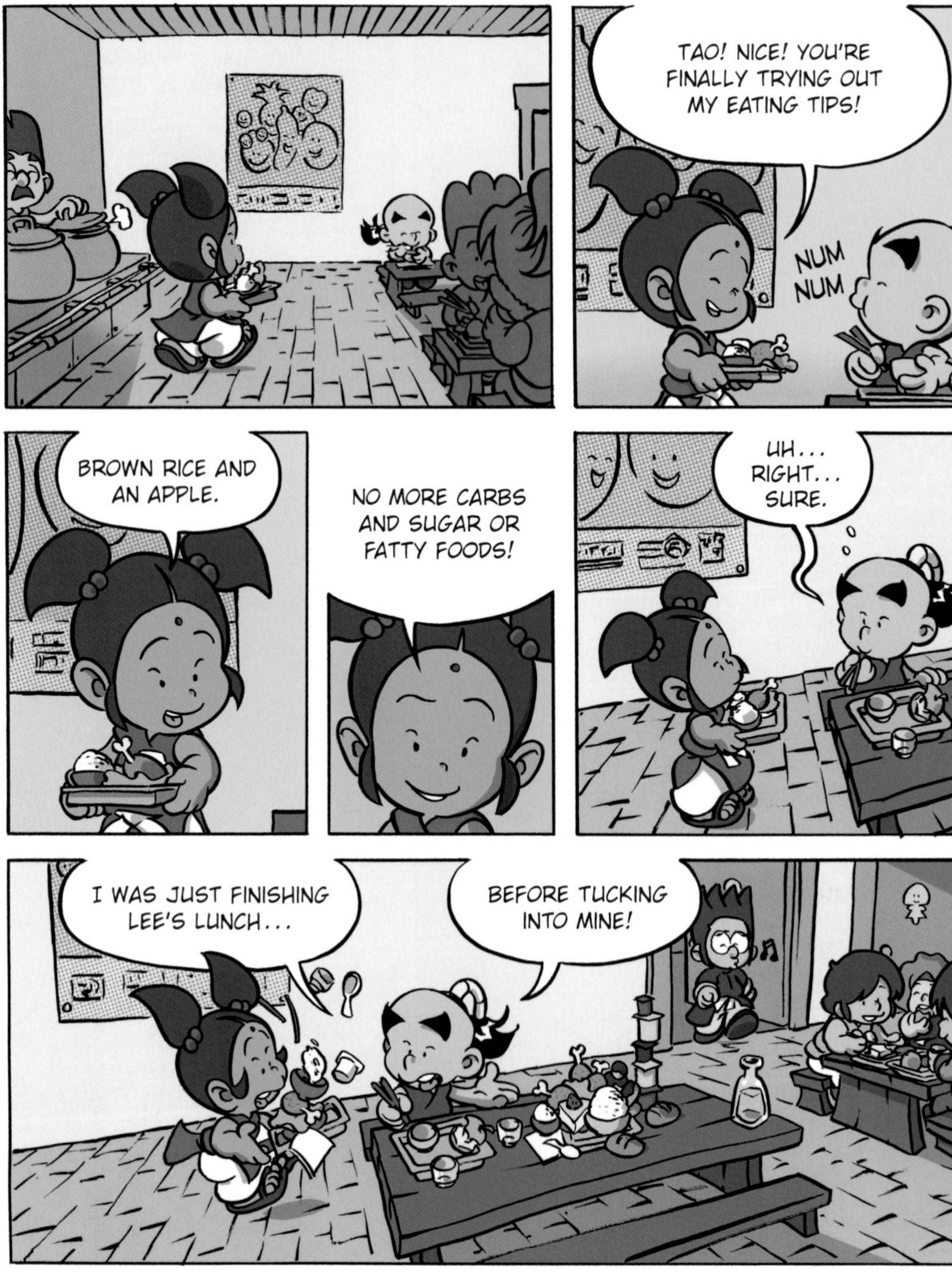
TAO! NICE! YOU'RE FINALLY TRYING OUT MY EATING TIPS!
NUM NUM
BROWN RICE AND AN APPLE.
NO MORE CARBS AND SUGAR OR FATTY FOODS!
UH... RIGHT... SURE.
I WAS JUST FINISHING LEE'S LUNCH...
BEFORE TUCKING INTO MINE!

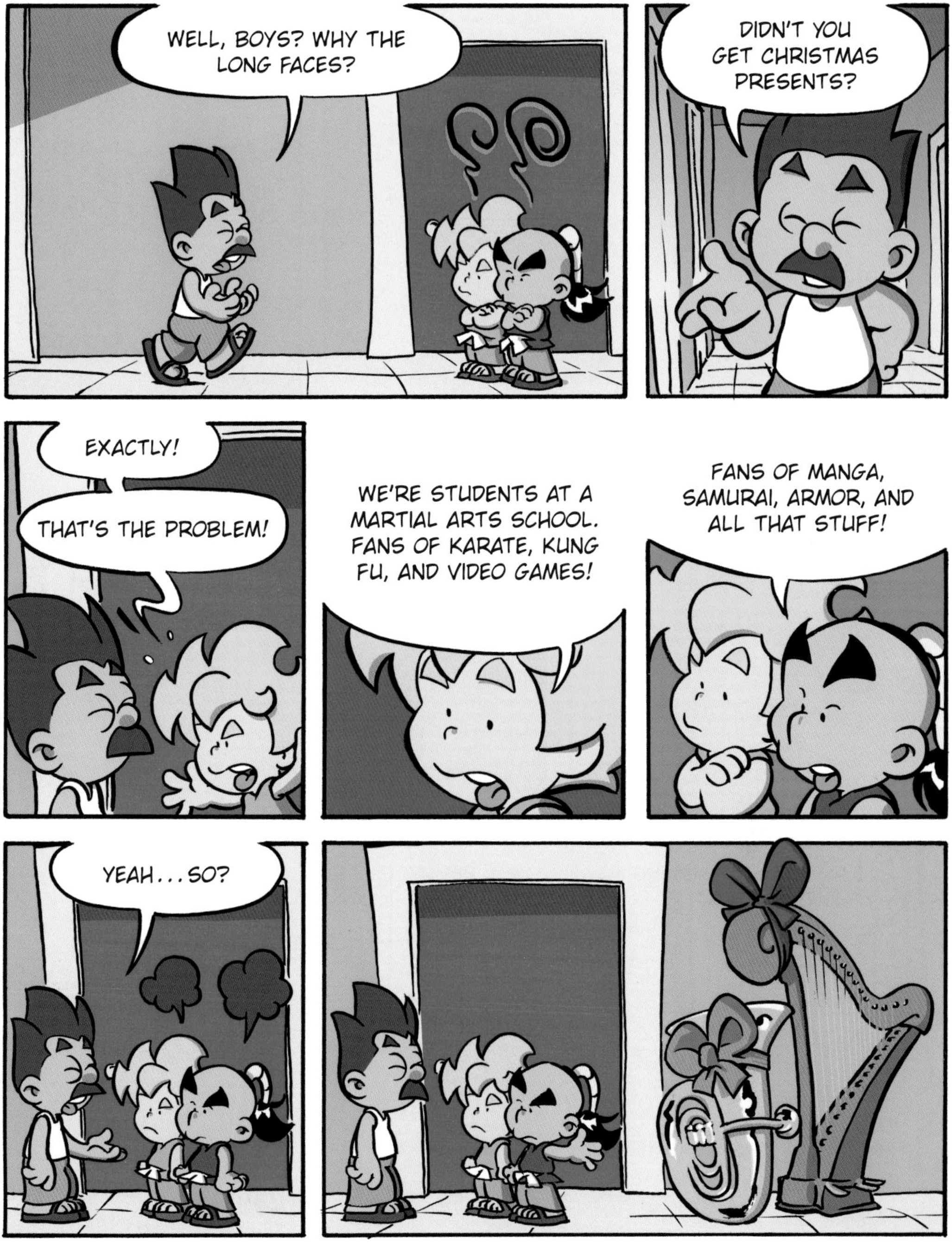
WELL, BOYS? WHY THE LONG FACES?
DIDN'T YOU GET CHRISTMAS PRESENTS?
EXACTLY!
THAT'S THE PROBLEM!
WE'RE STUDENTS AT A MARTIAL ARTS SCHOOL. FANS OF KARATE, KUNG FU, AND VIDEO GAMES!
FANS OF MANGA, SAMURAI, ARMOR, AND ALL THAT STUFF!
YEAH . . . SO?

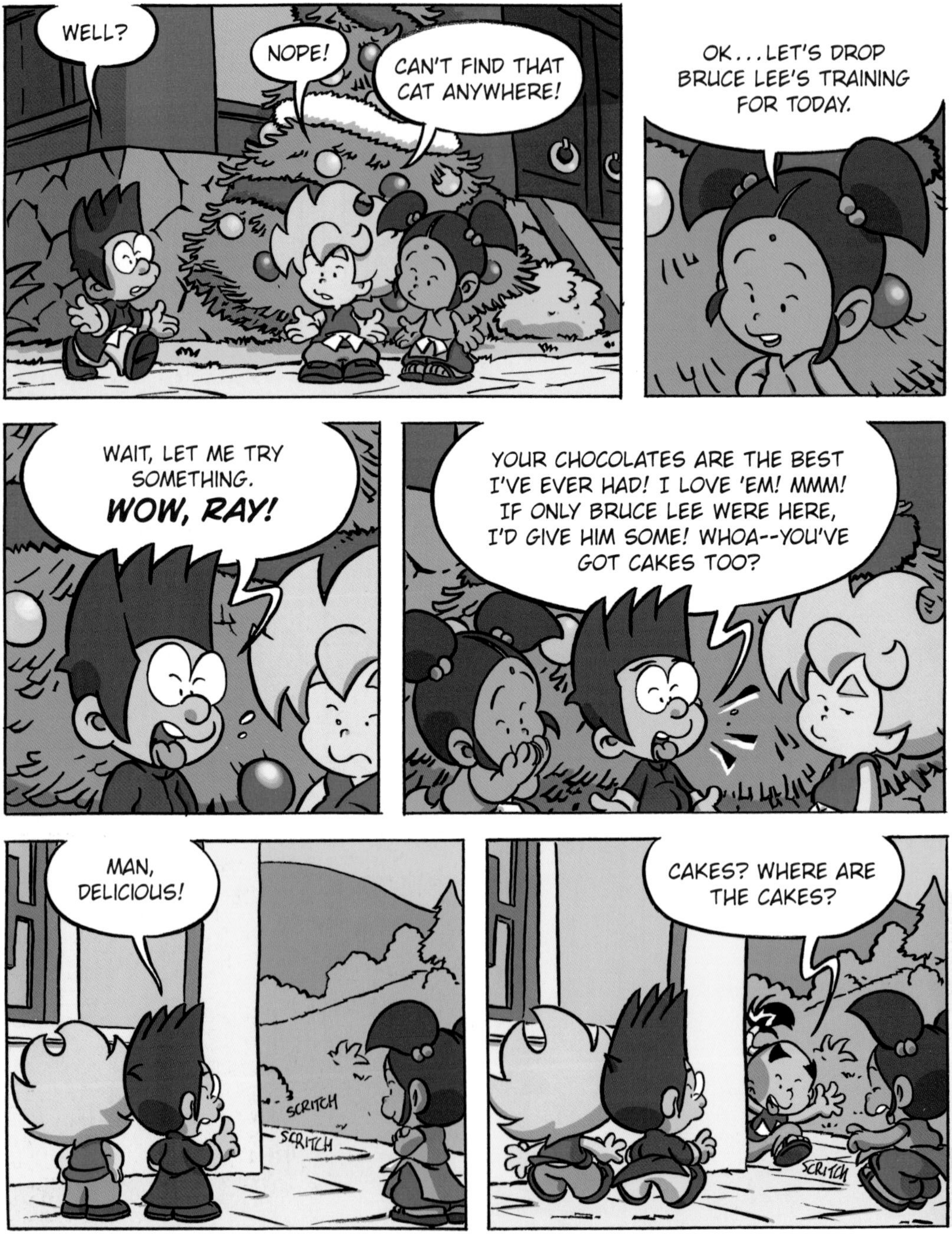
WELL?
NOPE!
CAN'T FIND THAT CAT ANYWHERE!
OK...LET'S DROP BRUCE LEE'S TRAINING FOR TODAY.
WAIT, LET ME TRY SOMETHING. **WOW, RAY!**
YOUR CHOCOLATES ARE THE BEST I'VE EVER HAD! I LOVE 'EM! MMM! IF ONLY BRUCE LEE WERE HERE, I'D GIVE HIM SOME! WHOA--YOU'VE GOT CAKES TOO?
MAN, DELICIOUS!
SCRITCH
SCRITCH
CAKES? WHERE ARE THE CAKES?
SCRITCH

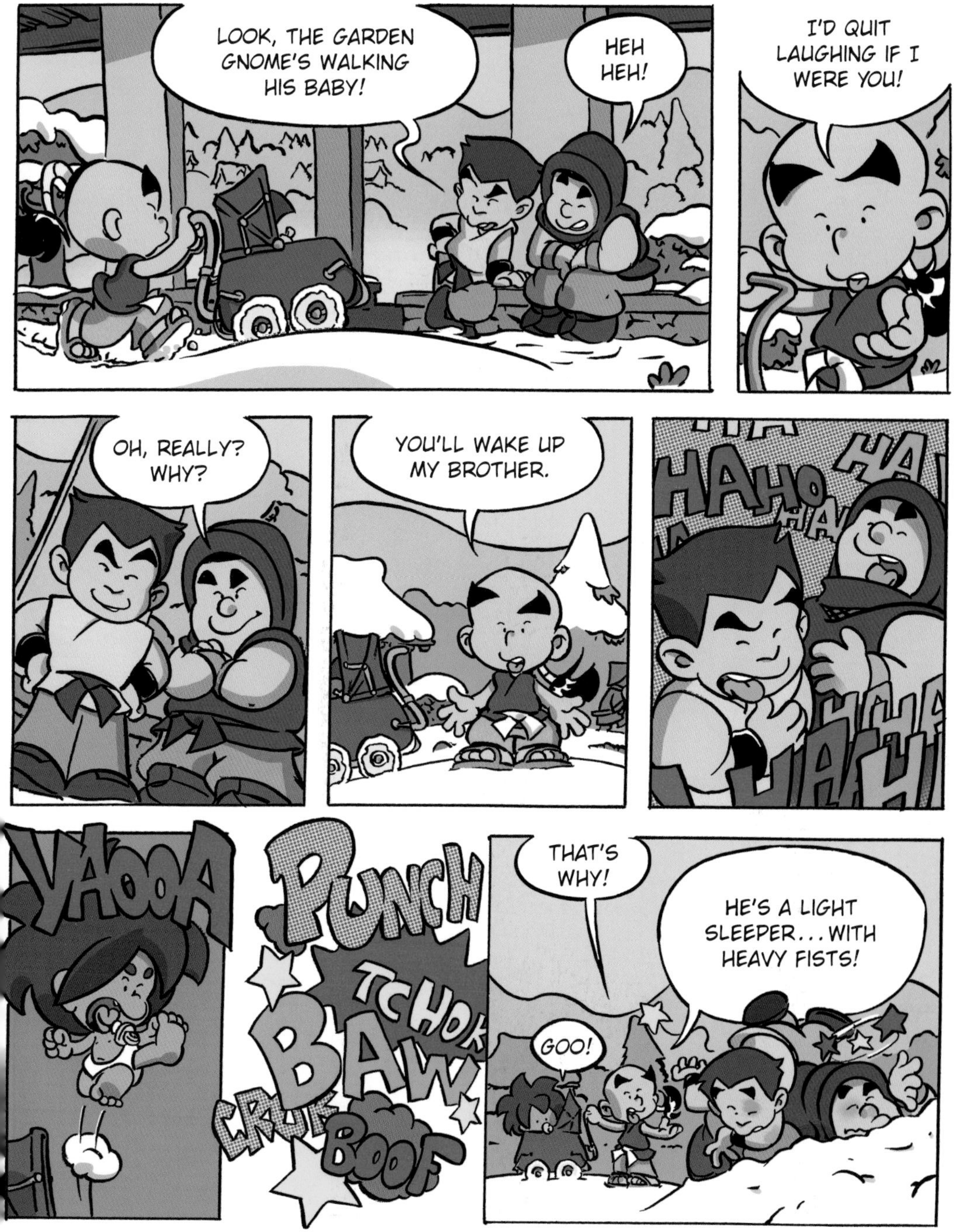
LOOK, THE GARDEN GNOME'S WALKING HIS BABY!
HEH HEH!
I'D QUIT LAUGHING IF I WERE YOU!
OH, REALLY? WHY?
YOU'LL WAKE UP MY BROTHER.
HA HO HA HA HA HA HA HA
YAOOA
PUNCH
TCHOK
BAW
CRUK
BOOF
THAT'S WHY!
HE'S A LIGHT SLEEPER... WITH HEAVY FISTS!
GOO!

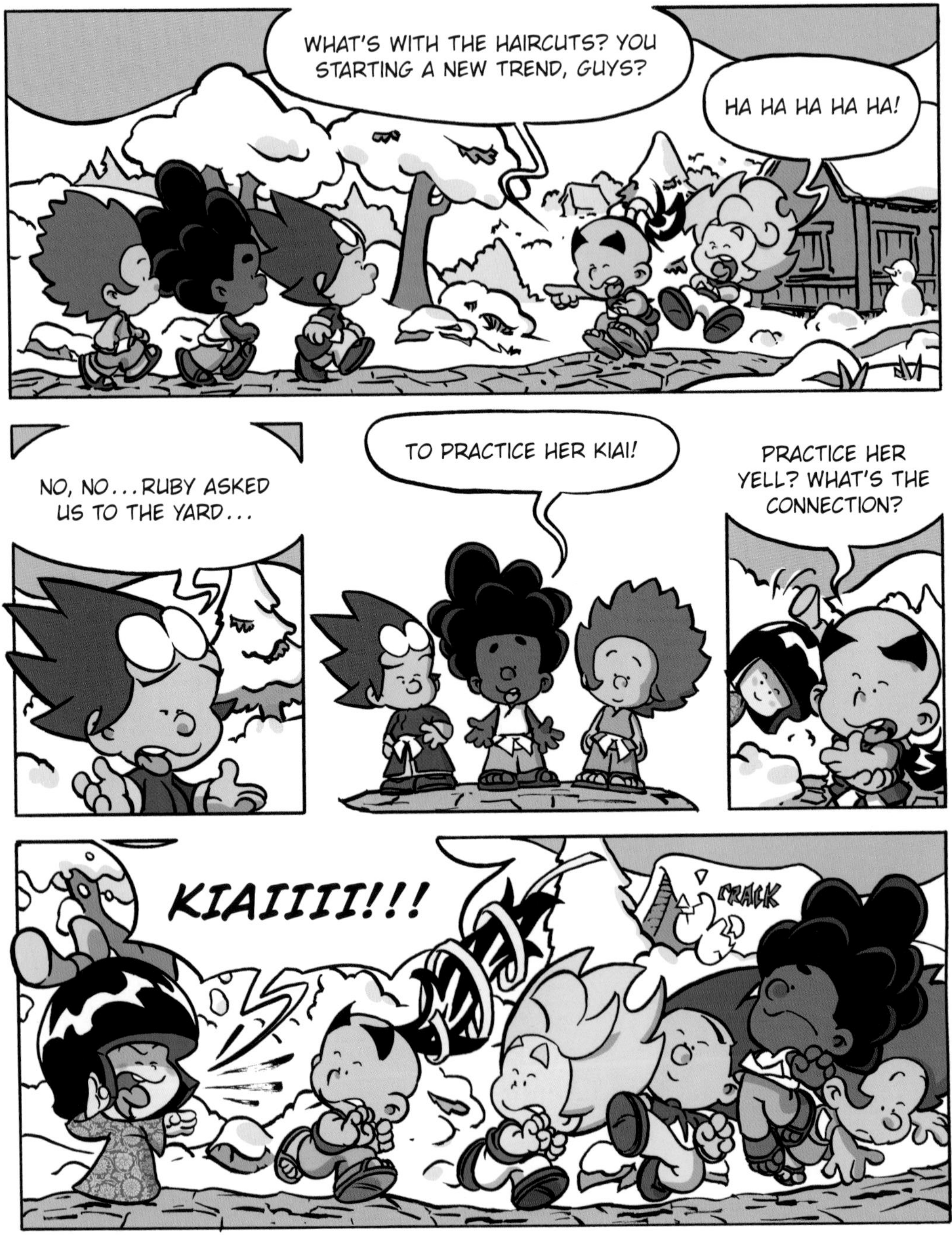
WHAT'S WITH THE HAIRCUTS? YOU STARTING A NEW TREND, GUYS?
HA HA HA HA HA!
NO, NO...RUBY ASKED US TO THE YARD...
TO PRACTICE HER KIAI!
PRACTICE HER YELL? WHAT'S THE CONNECTION?
KIAIIII!!!
CRACK

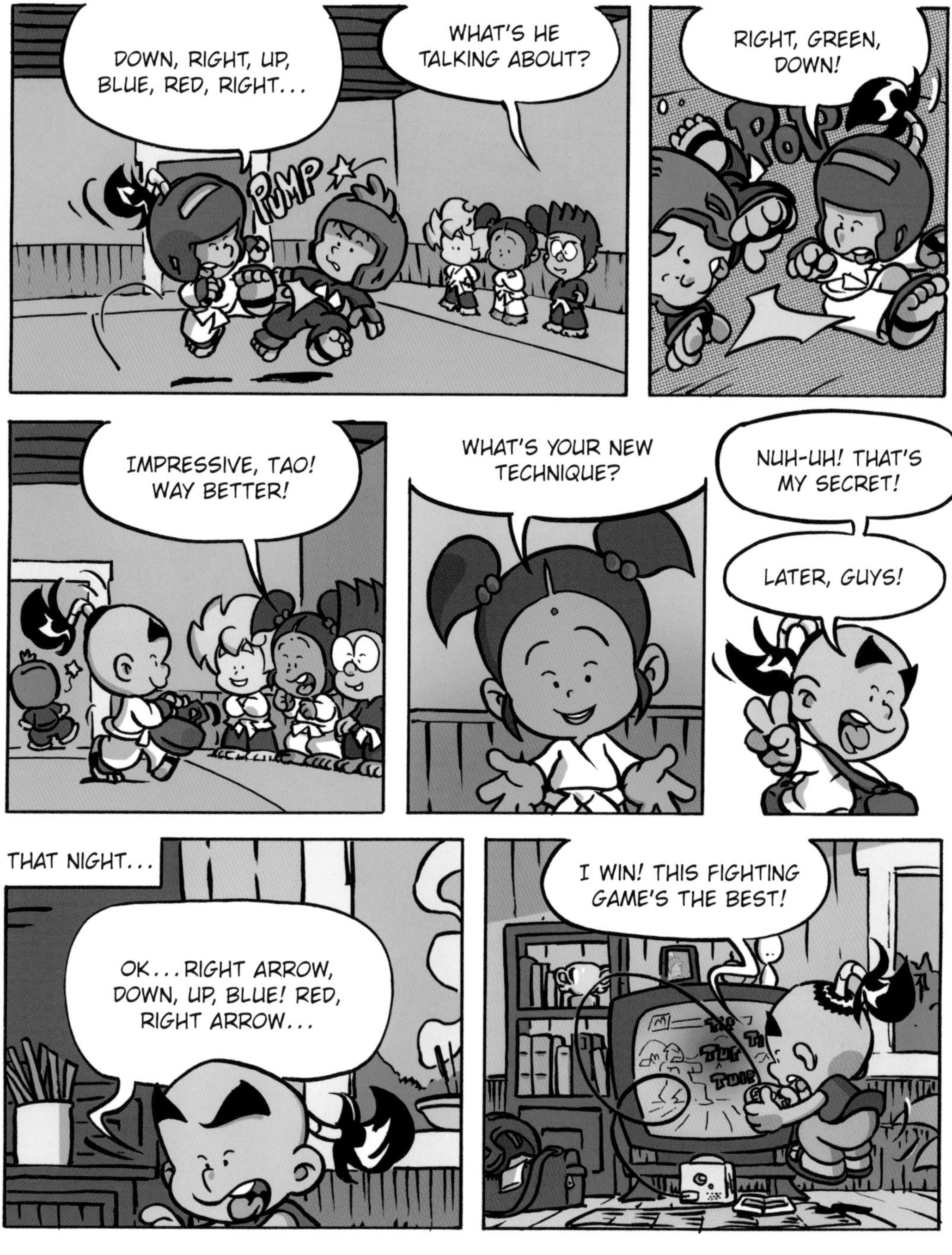
DOWN, RIGHT, UP, BLUE, RED, RIGHT...
PUMP
WHAT'S HE TALKING ABOUT?
RIGHT, GREEN, DOWN!
POP
IMPRESSIVE, TAO! WAY BETTER!
WHAT'S YOUR NEW TECHNIQUE?
NUH-UH! THAT'S MY SECRET!
LATER, GUYS!
THAT NIGHT...
OK...RIGHT ARROW, DOWN, UP, BLUE! RED, RIGHT ARROW...
I WIN! THIS FIGHTING GAME'S THE BEST!

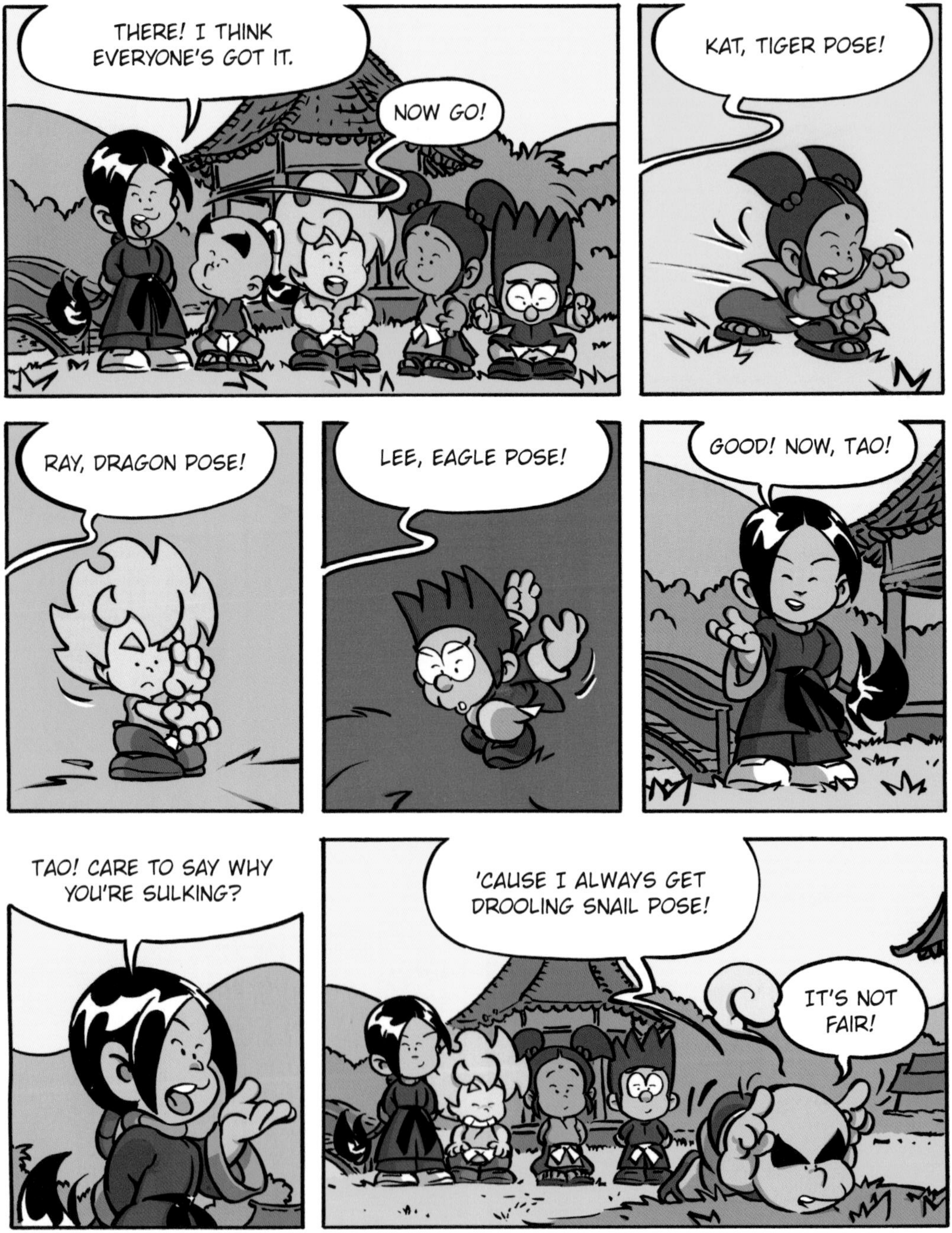
THERE! I THINK EVERYONE'S GOT IT.
NOW GO!
KAT, TIGER POSE!
RAY, DRAGON POSE!
LEE, EAGLE POSE!
GOOD! NOW, TAO!
TAO! CARE TO SAY WHY YOU'RE SULKING?
'CAUSE I ALWAYS GET DROOLING SNAIL POSE!
IT'S NOT FAIR!

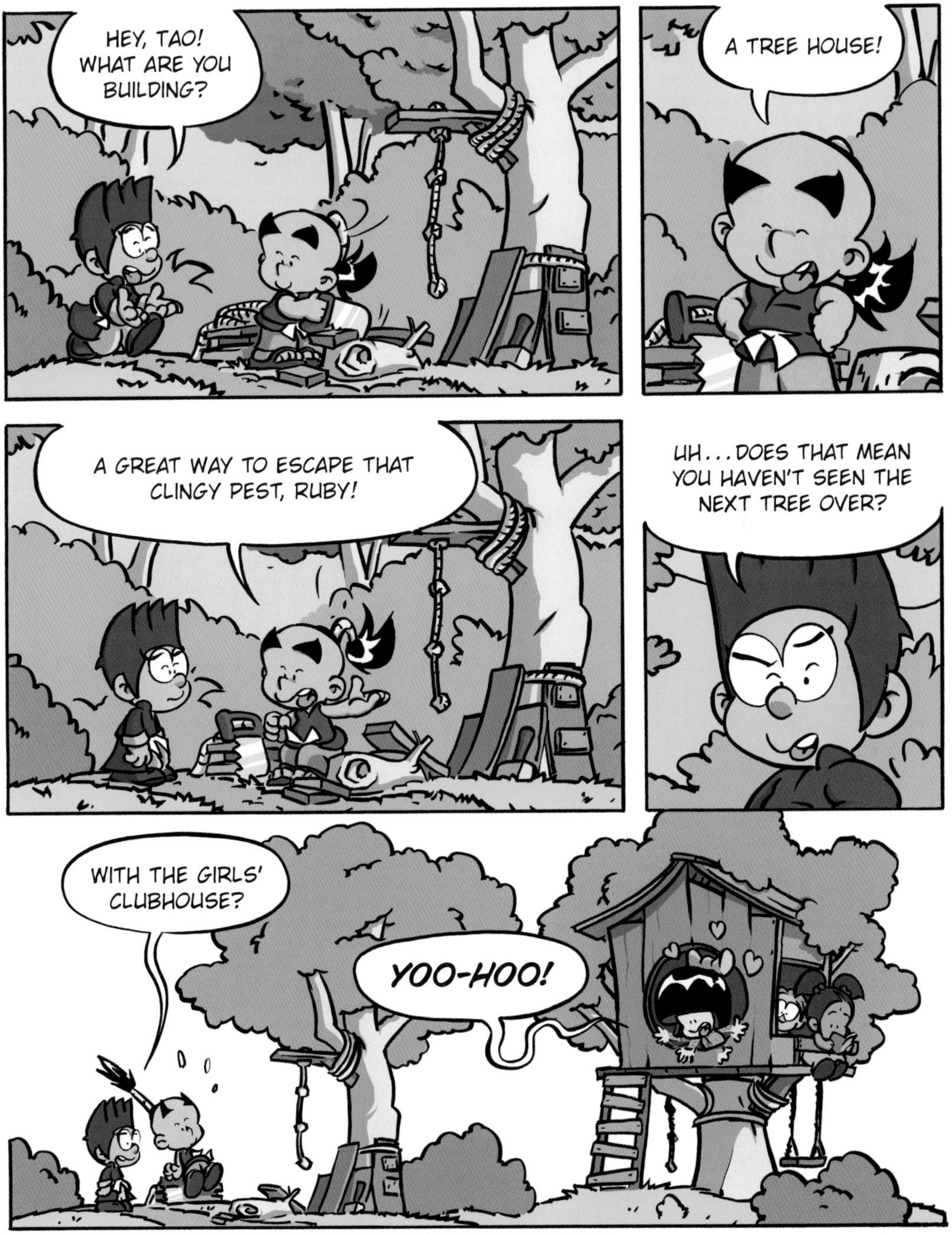
HEY, TAO! WHAT ARE YOU BUILDING?
A TREE HOUSE!
A GREAT WAY TO ESCAPE THAT CLINGY PEST, RUBY!
UH . . . DOES THAT MEAN YOU HAVEN'T SEEN THE NEXT TREE OVER?
WITH THE GIRLS' CLUBHOUSE?
YOO-HOO!

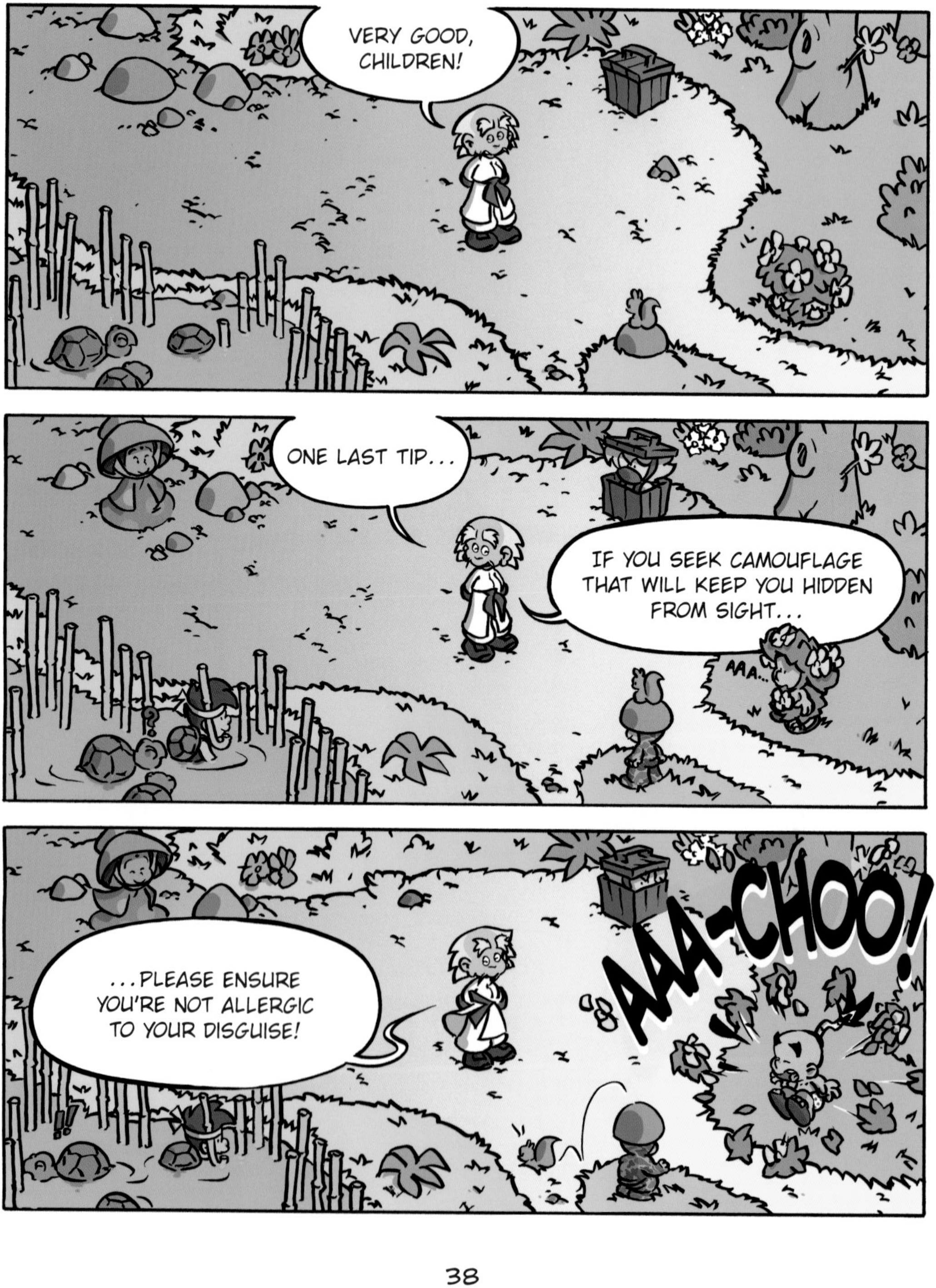
VERY GOOD, CHILDREN!
ONE LAST TIP...
IF YOU SEEK CAMOUFLAGE THAT WILL KEEP YOU HIDDEN FROM SIGHT...
AAA...
...PLEASE ENSURE YOU'RE NOT ALLERGIC TO YOUR DISGUISE!
AAA-CHOO!

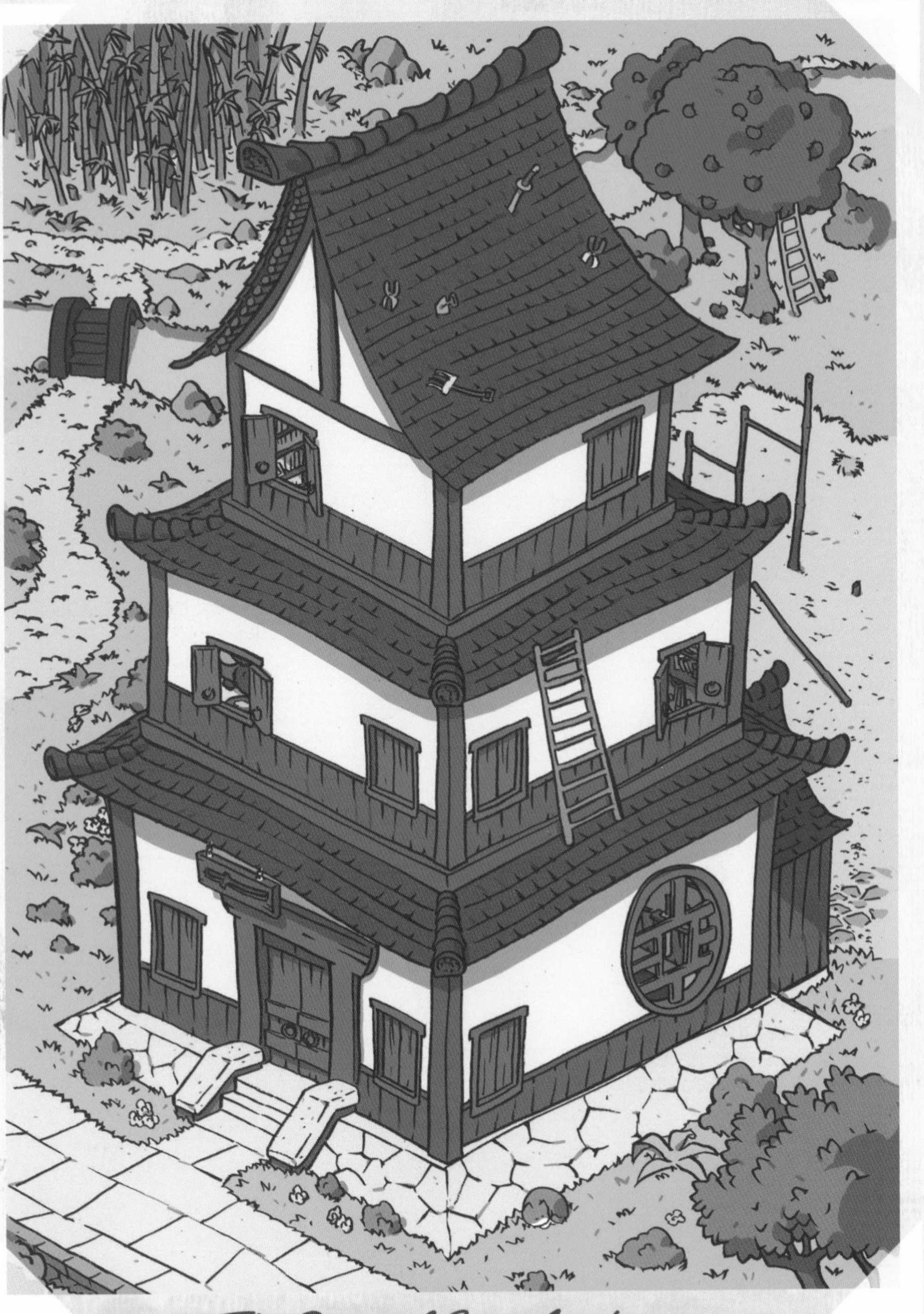

The Original Snow Academy

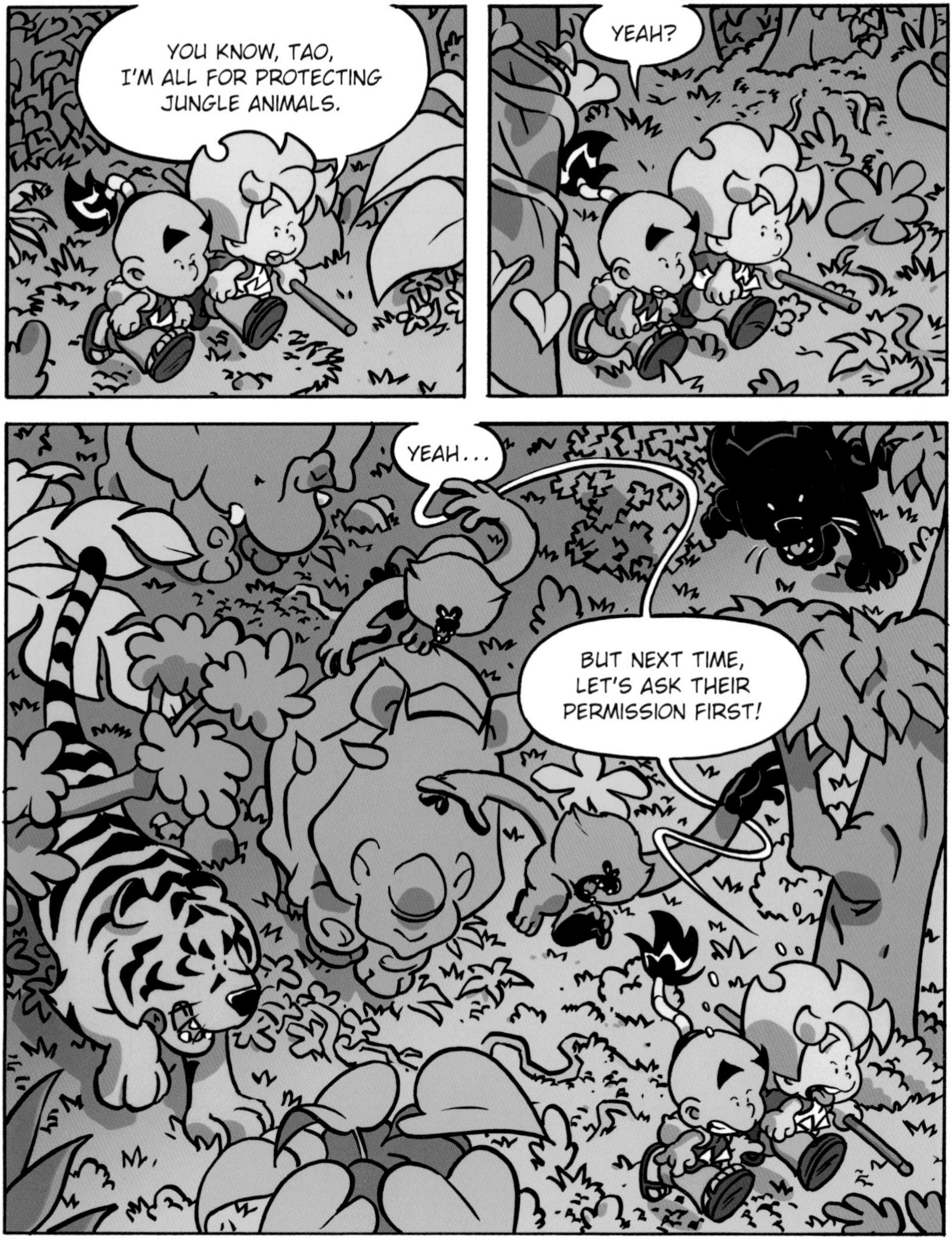
YOU KNOW, TAO, I'M ALL FOR PROTECTING JUNGLE ANIMALS.
YEAH?
YEAH...
BUT NEXT TIME, LET'S ASK THEIR PERMISSION FIRST!

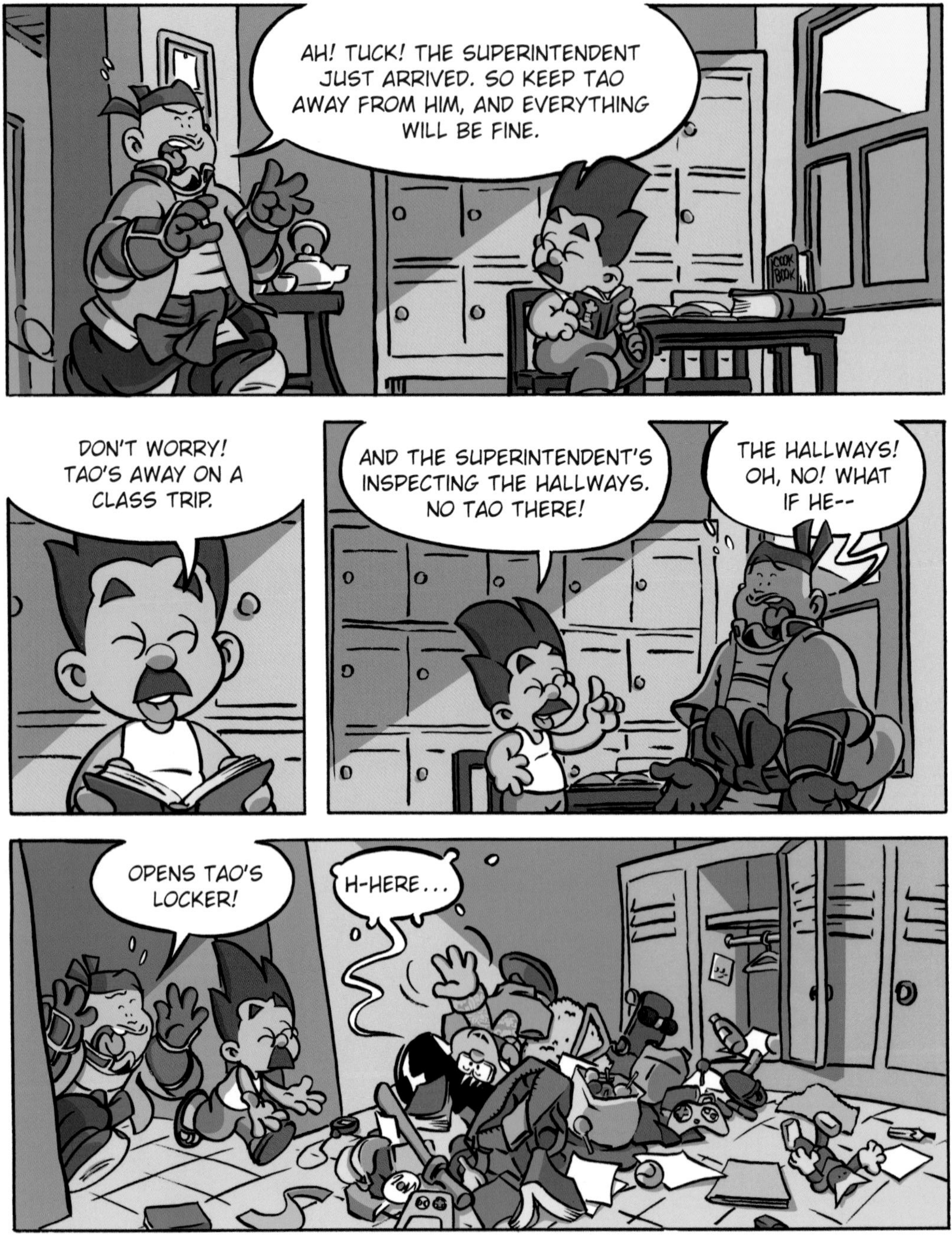
AH! TUCK! THE SUPERINTENDENT JUST ARRIVED. SO KEEP TAO AWAY FROM HIM, AND EVERYTHING WILL BE FINE.
COOK BOOK
DON'T WORRY! TAO'S AWAY ON A CLASS TRIP.
AND THE SUPERINTENDENT'S INSPECTING THE HALLWAYS. NO TAO THERE!
THE HALLWAYS! OH, NO! WHAT IF HE--
OPENS TAO'S LOCKER!
H-HERE...

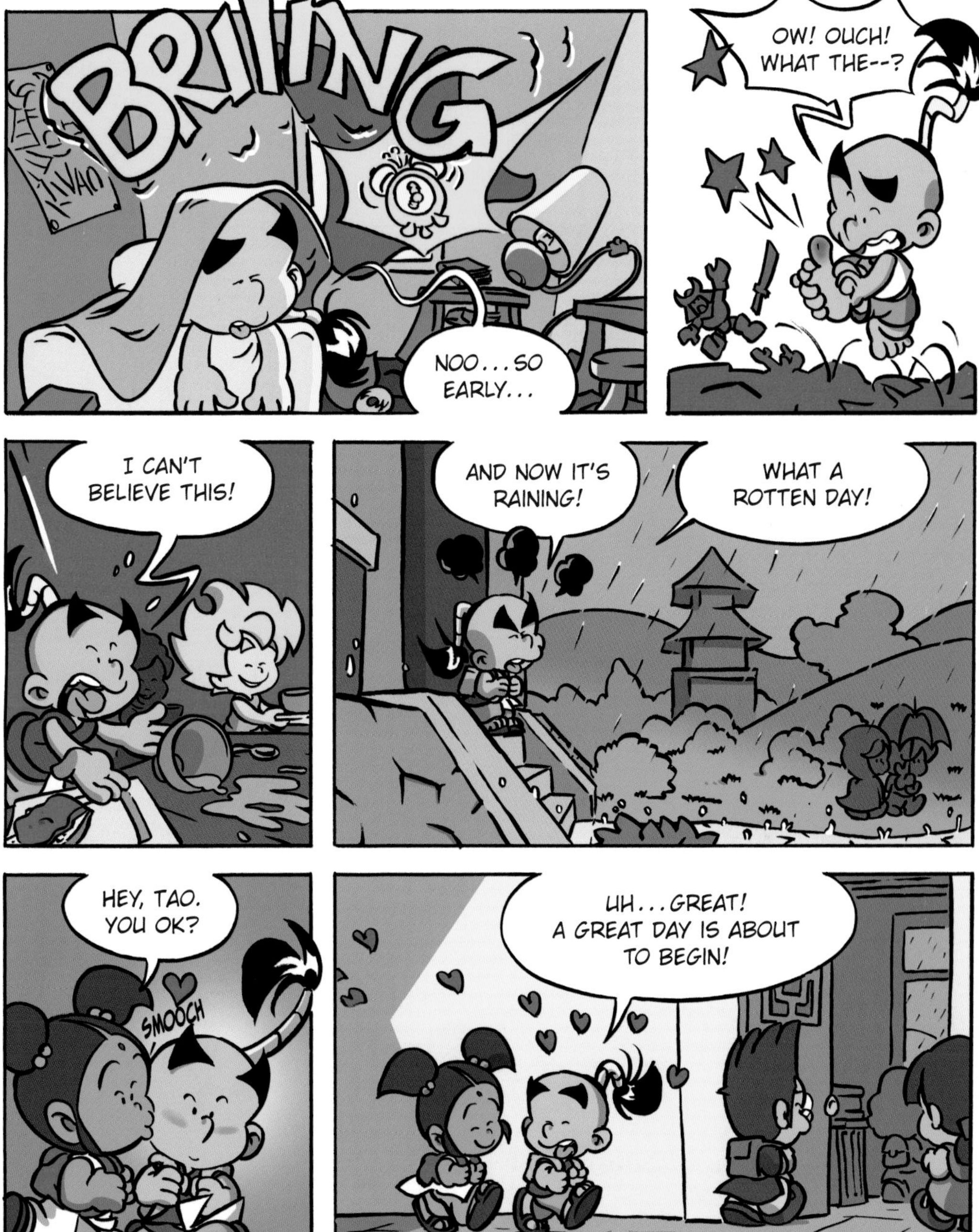
BRIIING
NOO...SO EARLY...
OW! OUCH! WHAT THE--?
I CAN'T BELIEVE THIS!
AND NOW IT'S RAINING!
WHAT A ROTTEN DAY!
HEY, TAO. YOU OK?
SMOOCH
UH...GREAT! A GREAT DAY IS ABOUT TO BEGIN!

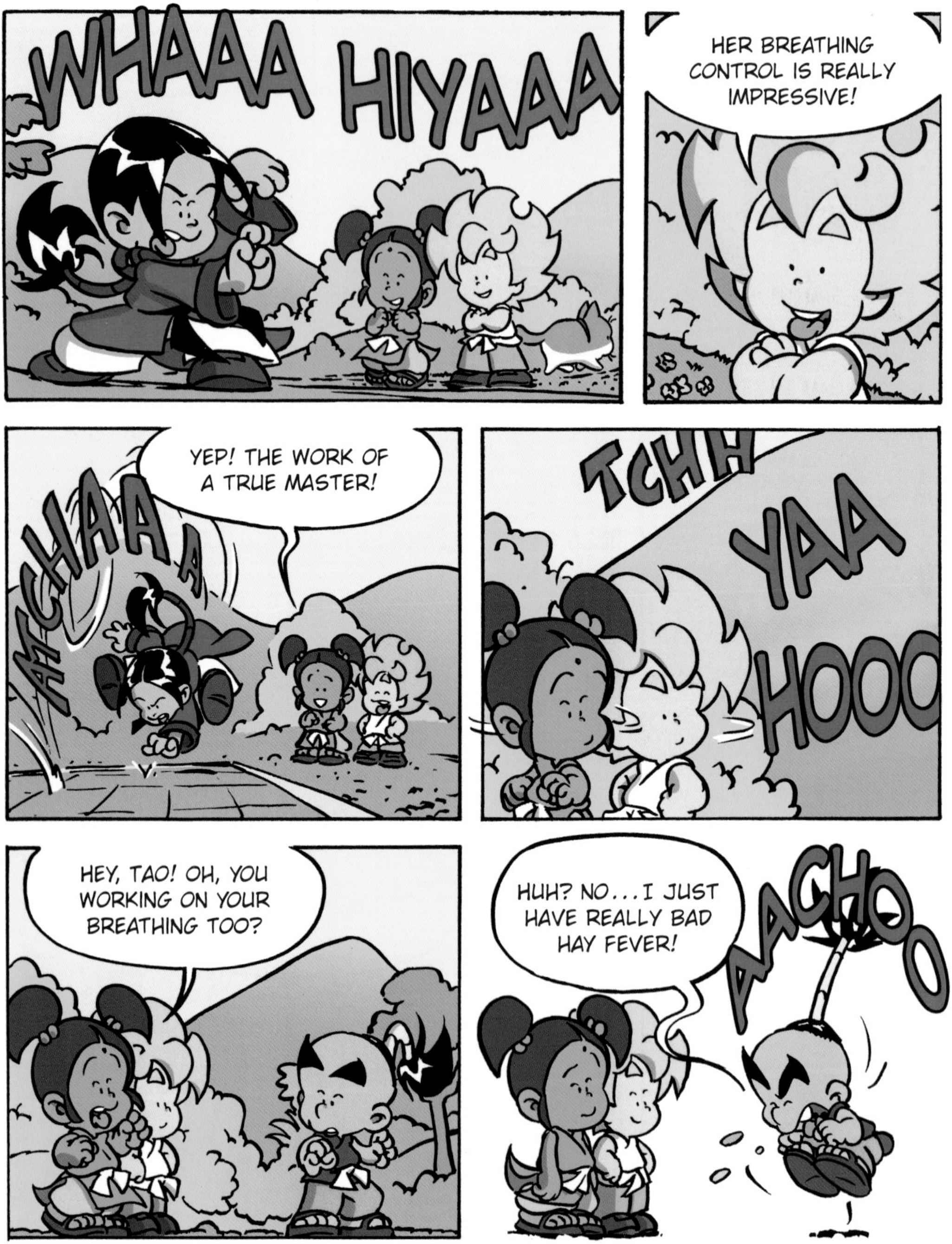
WHAAA HIYAAA
HER BREATHING CONTROL IS REALLY IMPRESSIVE!
ATCHAAAA
YEP! THE WORK OF A TRUE MASTER!
TCHH YAA HOOO
HEY, TAO! OH, YOU WORKING ON YOUR BREATHING TOO?
HUH? NO . . . I JUST HAVE REALLY BAD HAY FEVER!
AACHOO

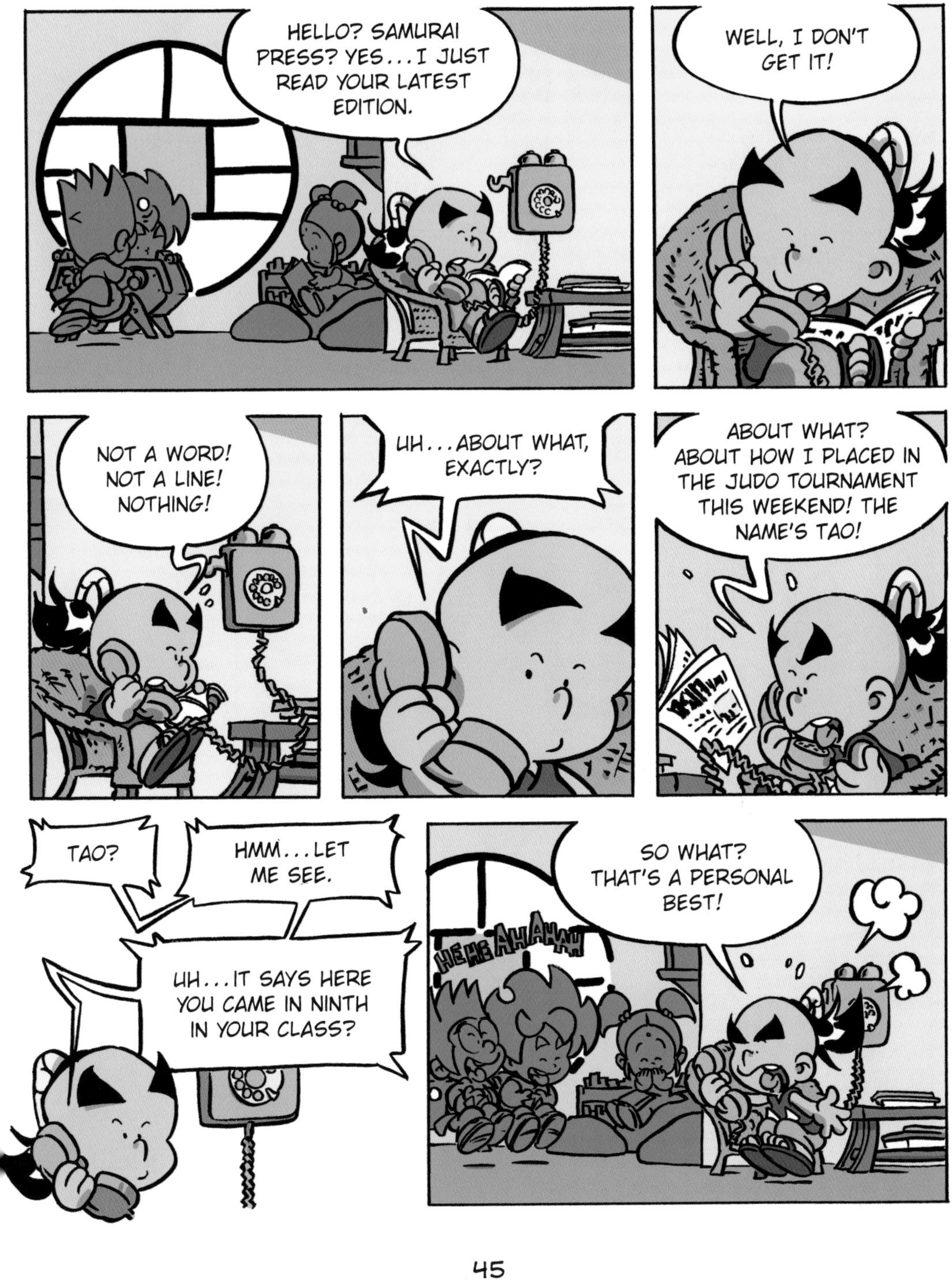
HELLO? SAMURAI PRESS? YES... I JUST READ YOUR LATEST EDITION.
WELL, I DON'T GET IT!
NOT A WORD! NOT A LINE! NOTHING!
UH... ABOUT WHAT, EXACTLY?
ABOUT WHAT? ABOUT HOW I PLACED IN THE JUDO TOURNAMENT THIS WEEKEND! THE NAME'S TAO!
TAO?
HMM... LET ME SEE.
UH... IT SAYS HERE YOU CAME IN NINTH IN YOUR CLASS?
SO WHAT? THAT'S A PERSONAL BEST!
HEHEHAHAHAHAH

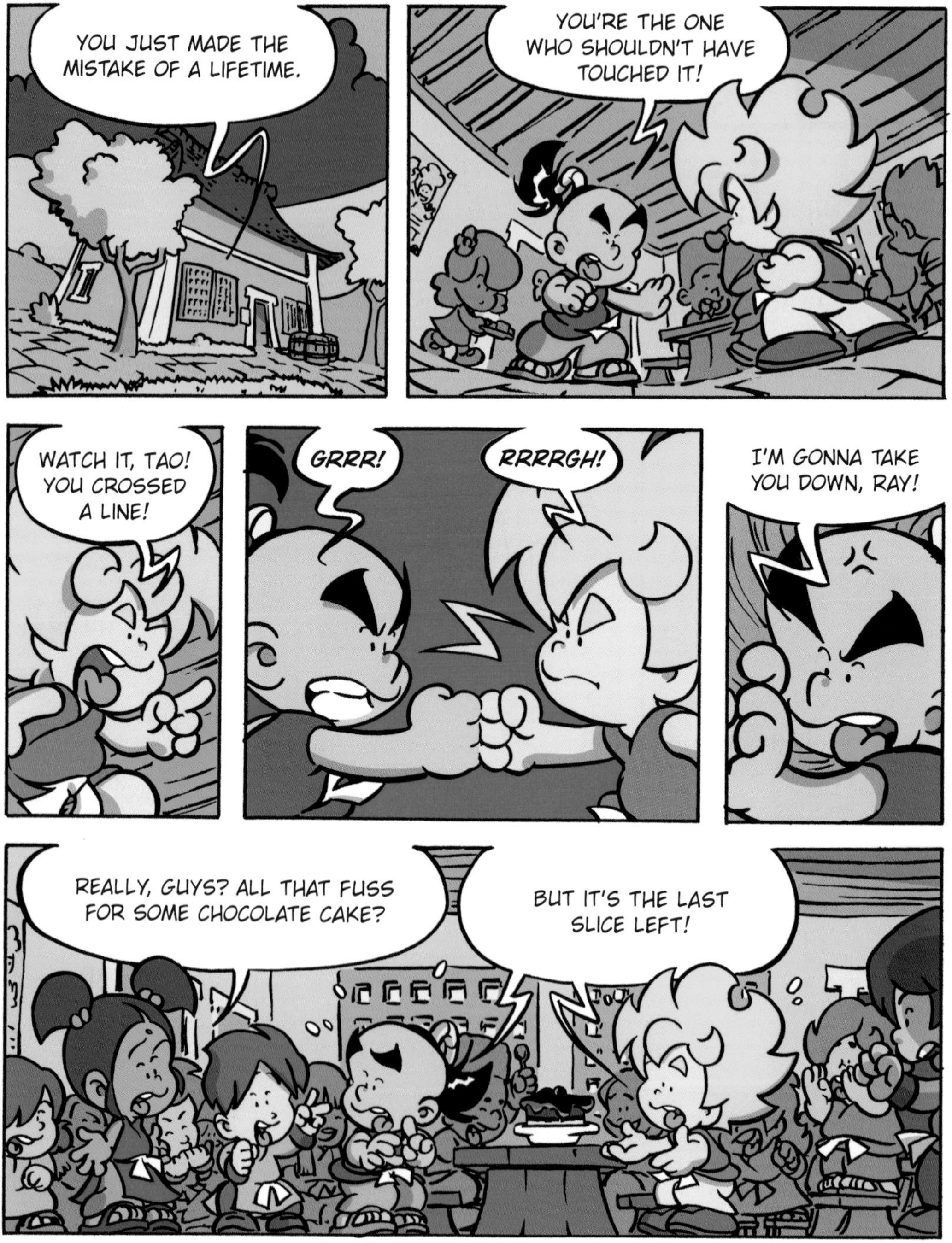

YOU JUST MADE THE MISTAKE OF A LIFETIME.
YOU'RE THE ONE WHO SHOULDN'T HAVE TOUCHED IT!
WATCH IT, TAO! YOU CROSSED A LINE!
GRRR!
RRRRGH!
I'M GONNA TAKE YOU DOWN, RAY!
REALLY, GUYS? ALL THAT FUSS FOR SOME CHOCOLATE CAKE?
BUT IT'S THE LAST SLICE LEFT!

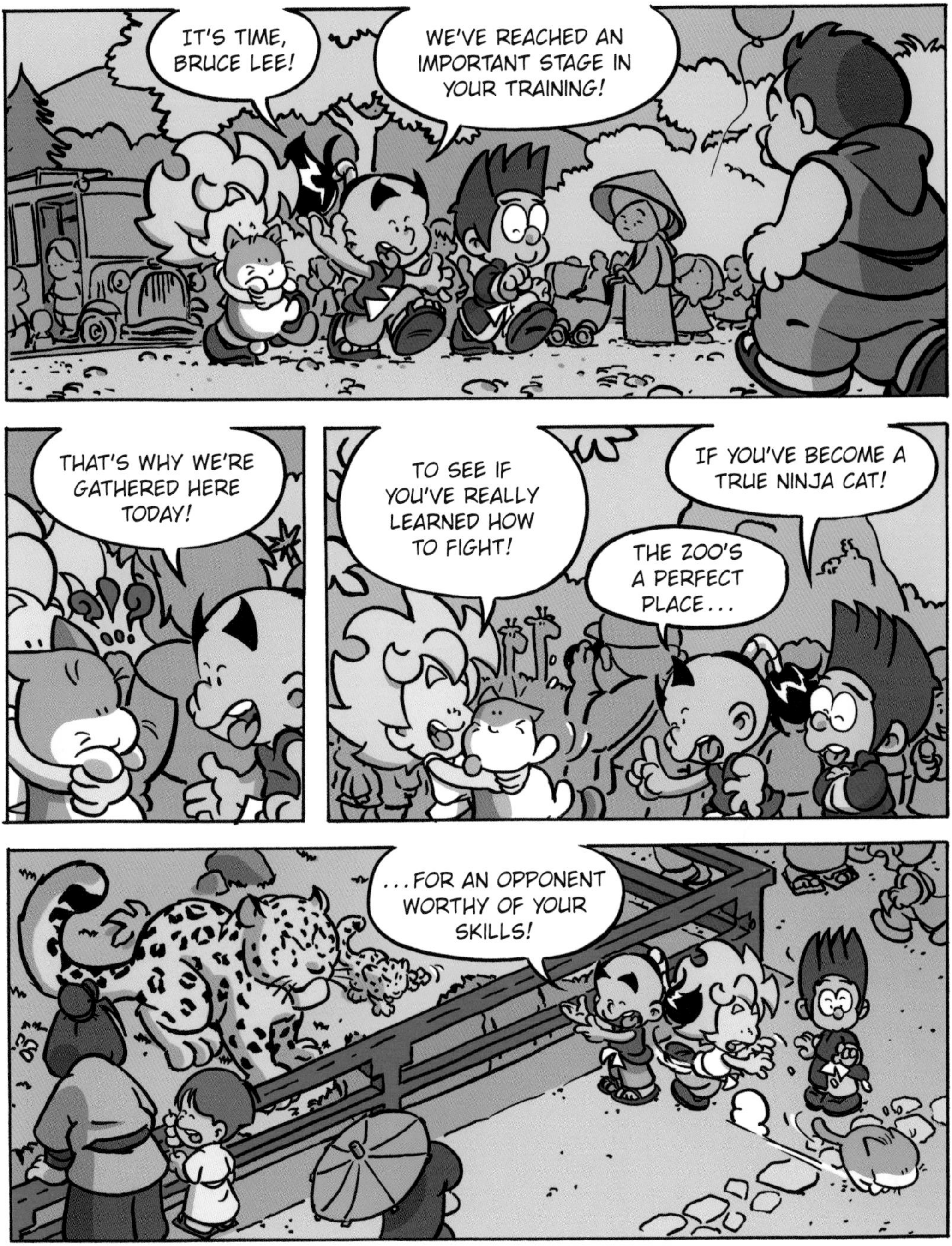
IT'S TIME, BRUCE LEE!
WE'VE REACHED AN IMPORTANT STAGE IN YOUR TRAINING!
THAT'S WHY WE'RE GATHERED HERE TODAY!
TO SEE IF YOU'VE REALLY LEARNED HOW TO FIGHT!
IF YOU'VE BECOME A TRUE NINJA CAT!
THE ZOO'S A PERFECT PLACE...
...FOR AN OPPONENT WORTHY OF YOUR SKILLS!

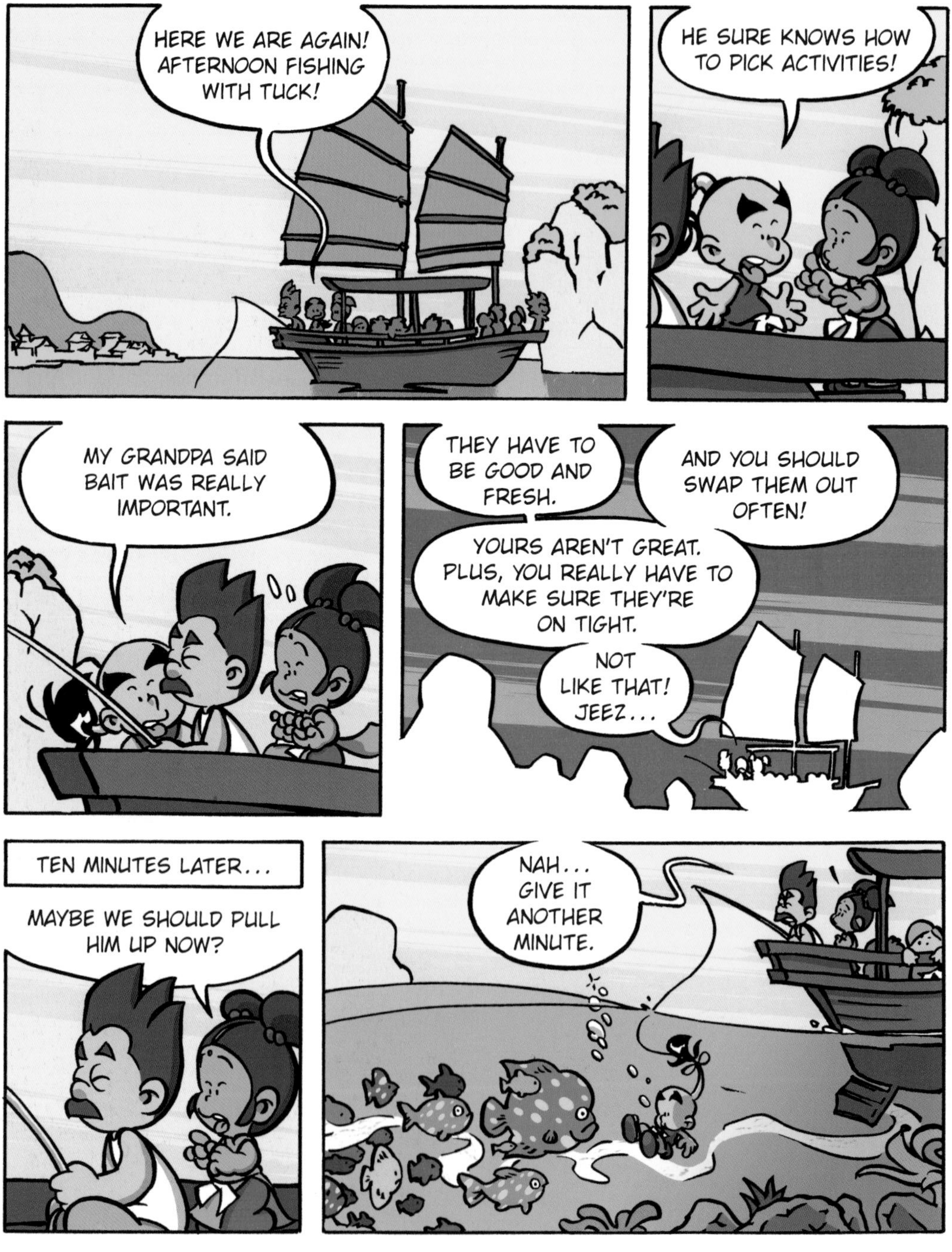
HERE WE ARE AGAIN! AFTERNOON FISHING WITH TUCK!
HE SURE KNOWS HOW TO PICK ACTIVITIES!
MY GRANDPA SAID BAIT WAS REALLY IMPORTANT.
THEY HAVE TO BE GOOD AND FRESH.
AND YOU SHOULD SWAP THEM OUT OFTEN!
YOURS AREN'T GREAT. PLUS, YOU REALLY HAVE TO MAKE SURE THEY'RE ON TIGHT.
NOT LIKE THAT! JEEZ...
TEN MINUTES LATER...
MAYBE WE SHOULD PULL HIM UP NOW?
NAH... GIVE IT ANOTHER MINUTE.

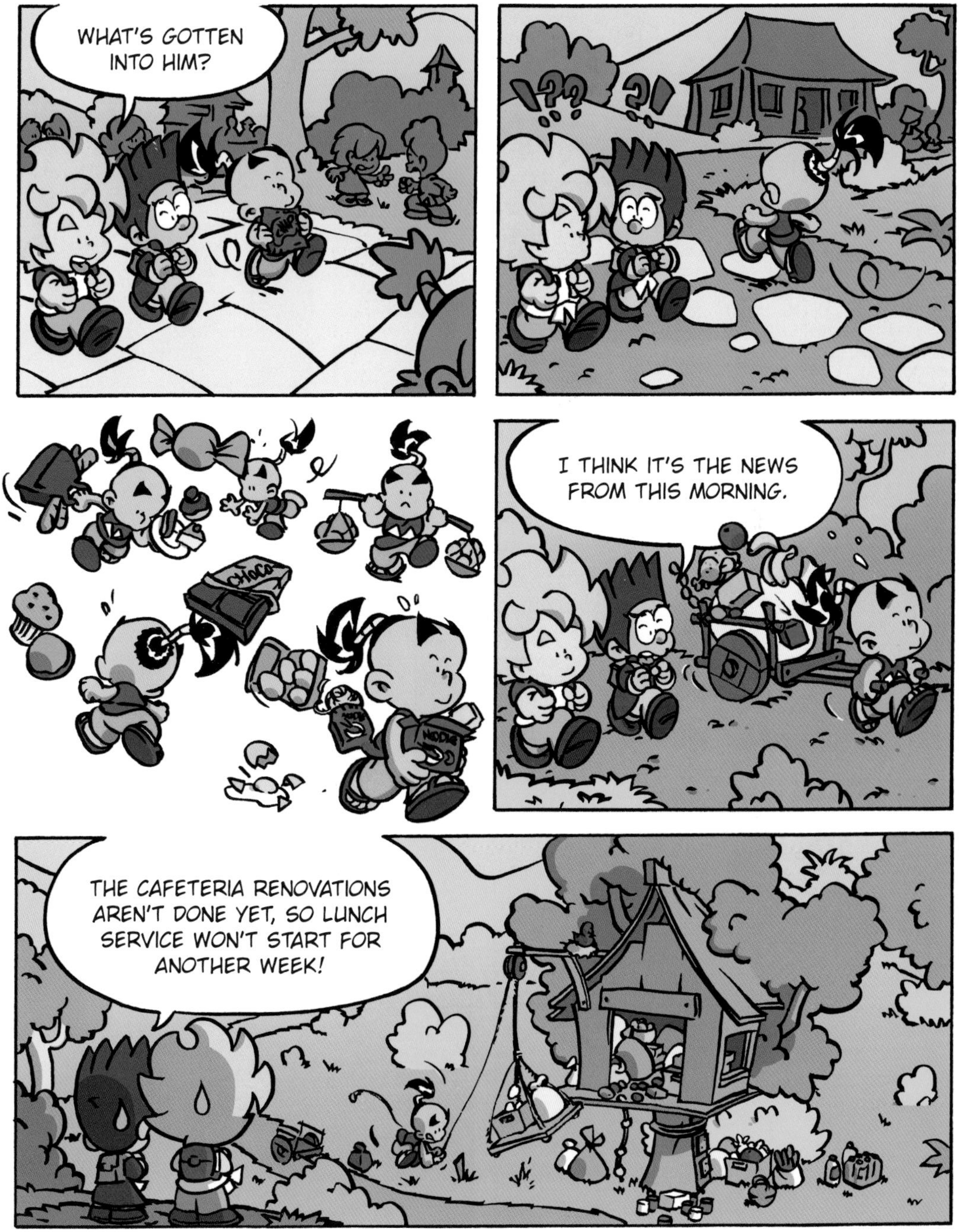
WHAT'S GOTTEN INTO HIM?
!??
?!
CHOCO
I THINK IT'S THE NEWS FROM THIS MORNING.
THE CAFETERIA RENOVATIONS AREN'T DONE YET, SO LUNCH SERVICE WON'T START FOR ANOTHER WEEK!

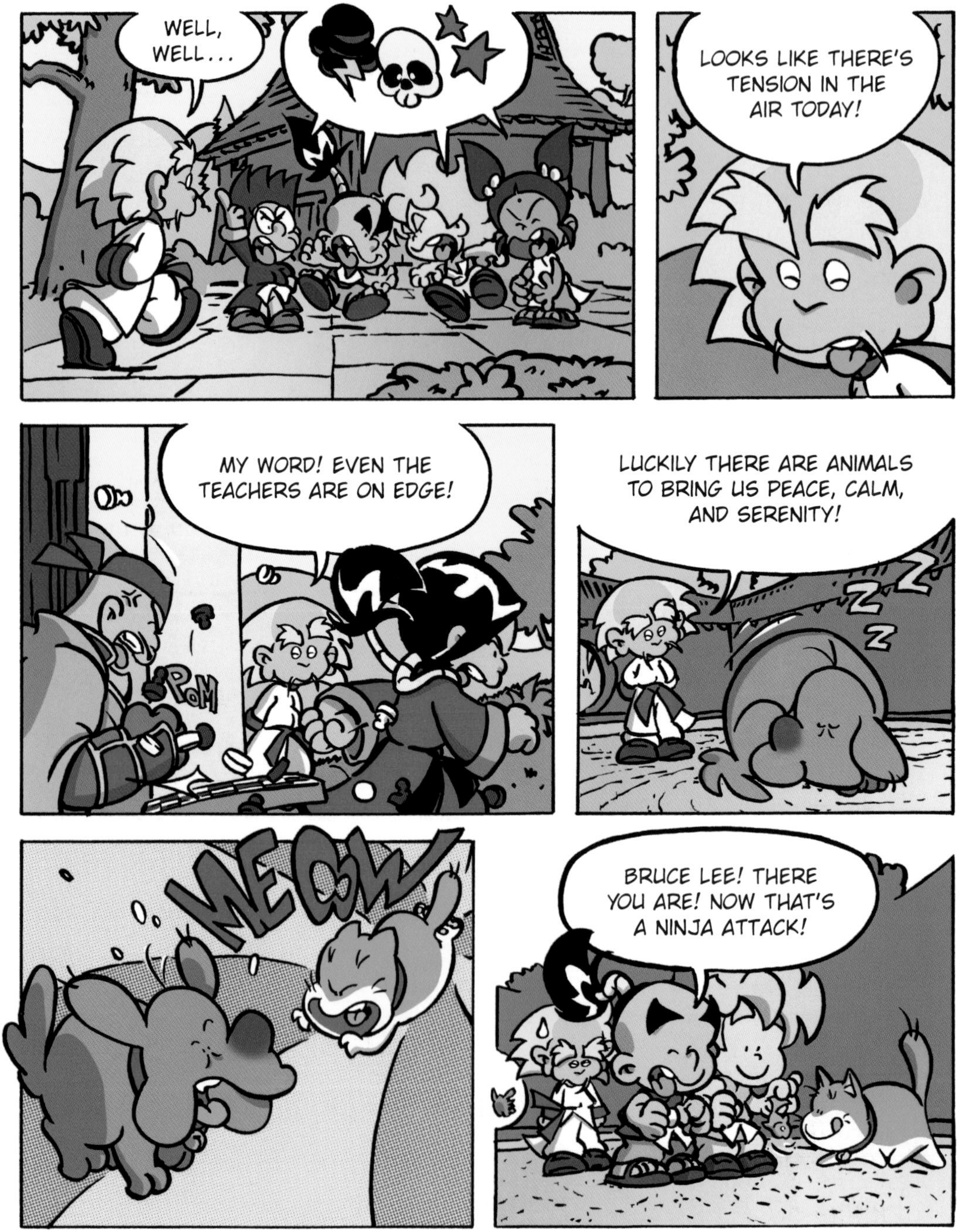
WELL, WELL...
LOOKS LIKE THERE'S TENSION IN THE AIR TODAY!
MY WORD! EVEN THE TEACHERS ARE ON EDGE!
POM
LUCKILY THERE ARE ANIMALS TO BRING US PEACE, CALM, AND SERENITY!
Z Z Z Z
MEOW
BRUCE LEE! THERE YOU ARE! NOW THAT'S A NINJA ATTACK!

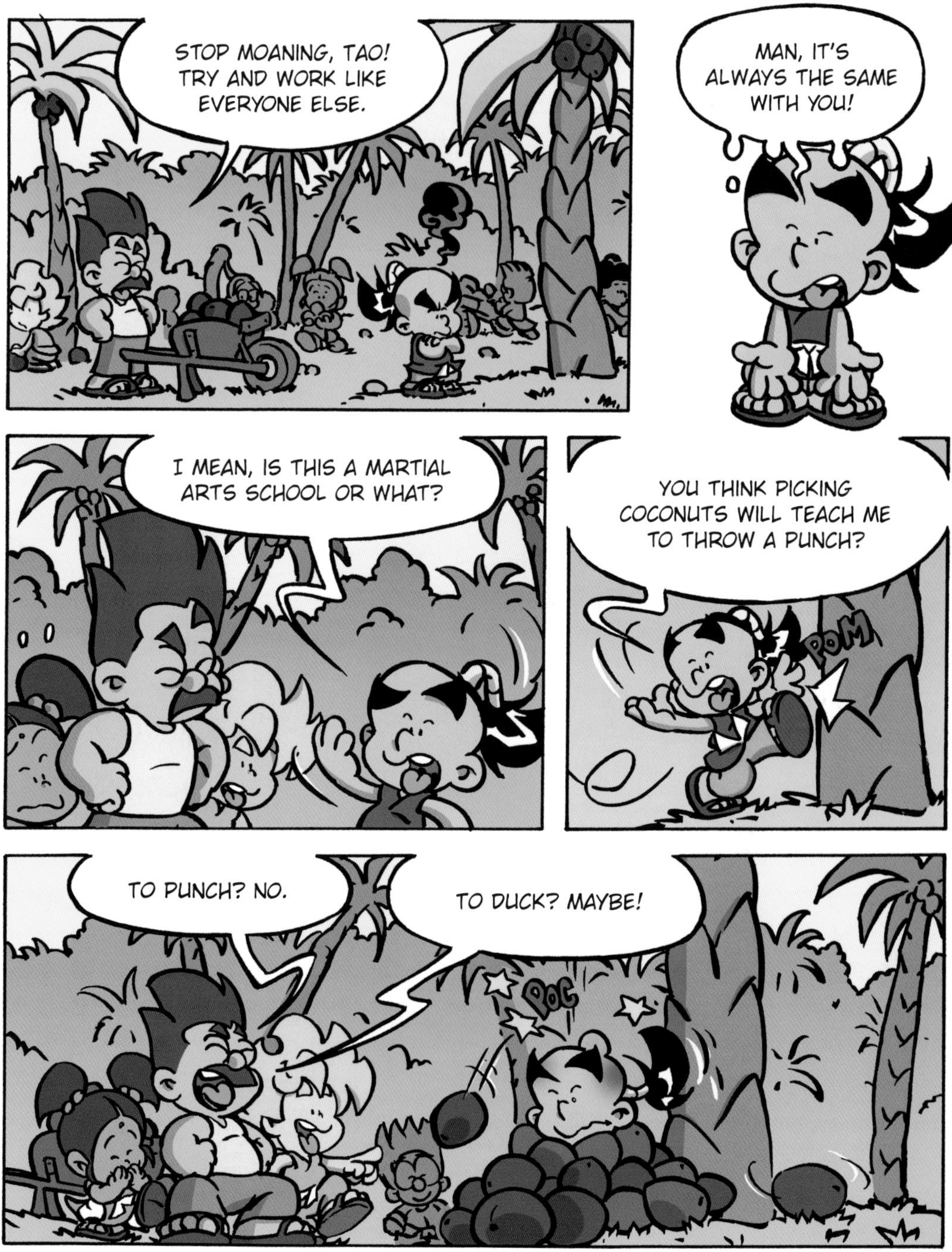
STOP MOANING, TAO! TRY AND WORK LIKE EVERYONE ELSE.
MAN, IT'S ALWAYS THE SAME WITH YOU!
I MEAN, IS THIS A MARTIAL ARTS SCHOOL OR WHAT?
YOU THINK PICKING COCONUTS WILL TEACH ME TO THROW A PUNCH?
POM
TO PUNCH? NO.
TO DUCK? MAYBE!
POC

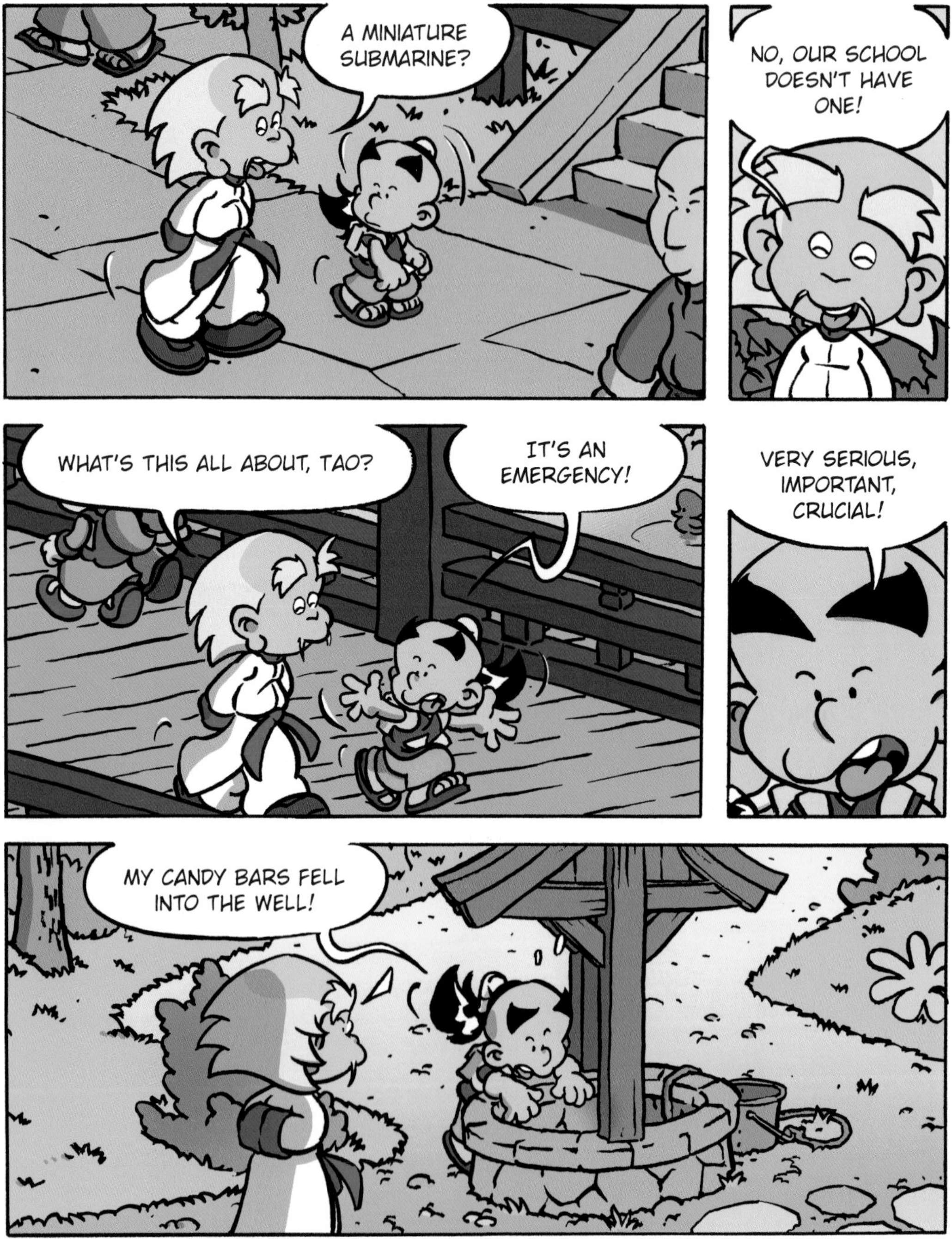
A MINIATURE SUBMARINE?
NO, OUR SCHOOL DOESN'T HAVE ONE!
WHAT'S THIS ALL ABOUT, TAO?
IT'S AN EMERGENCY!
VERY SERIOUS, IMPORTANT, CRUCIAL!
MY CANDY BARS FELL INTO THE WELL!

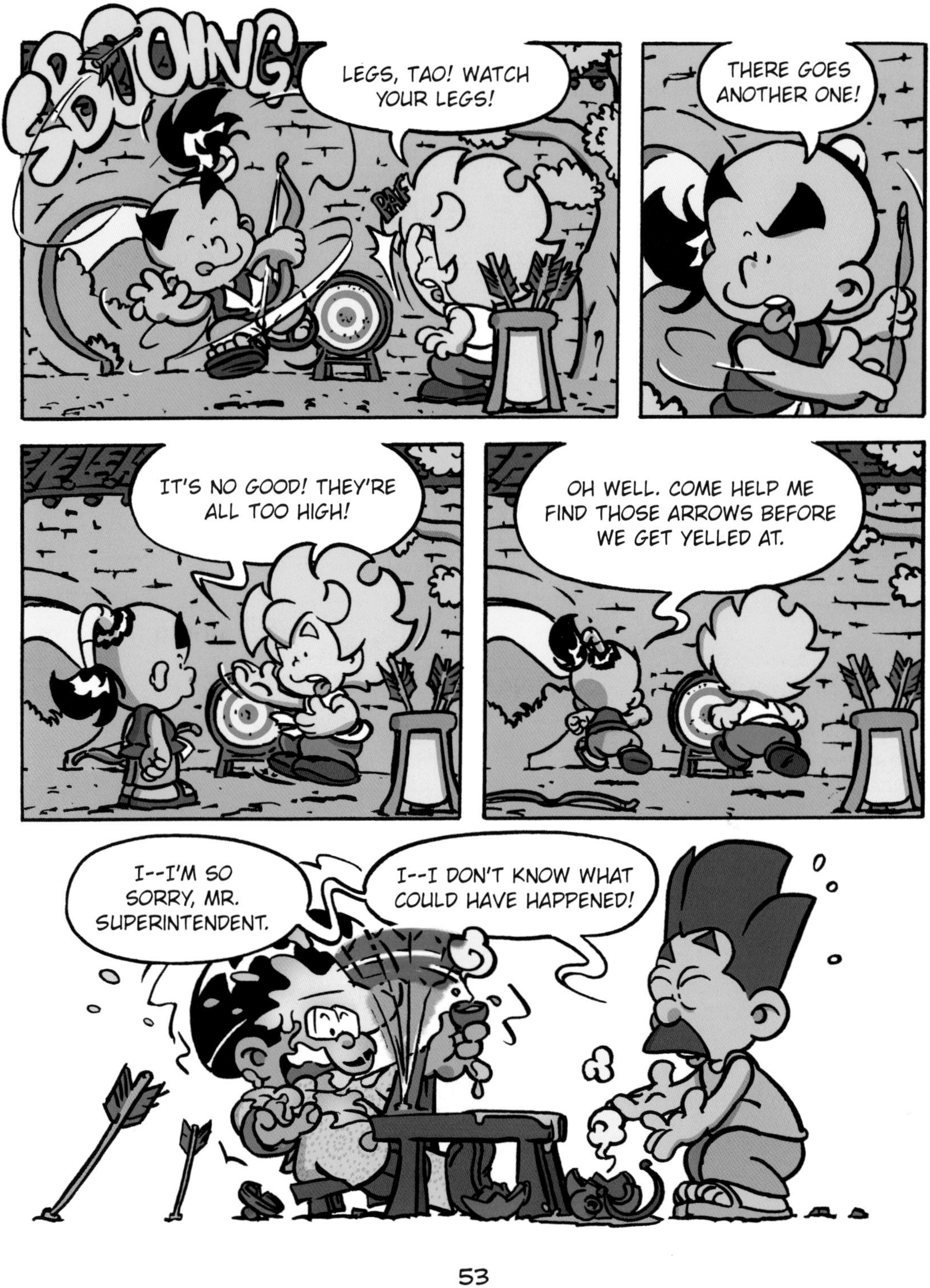
SBOING
LEGS, TAO! WATCH YOUR LEGS!
PAF
THERE GOES ANOTHER ONE!
IT'S NO GOOD! THEY'RE ALL TOO HIGH!
OH WELL. COME HELP ME FIND THOSE ARROWS BEFORE WE GET YELLED AT.
I--I'M SO SORRY, MR. SUPERINTENDENT.
I--I DON'T KNOW WHAT COULD HAVE HAPPENED!

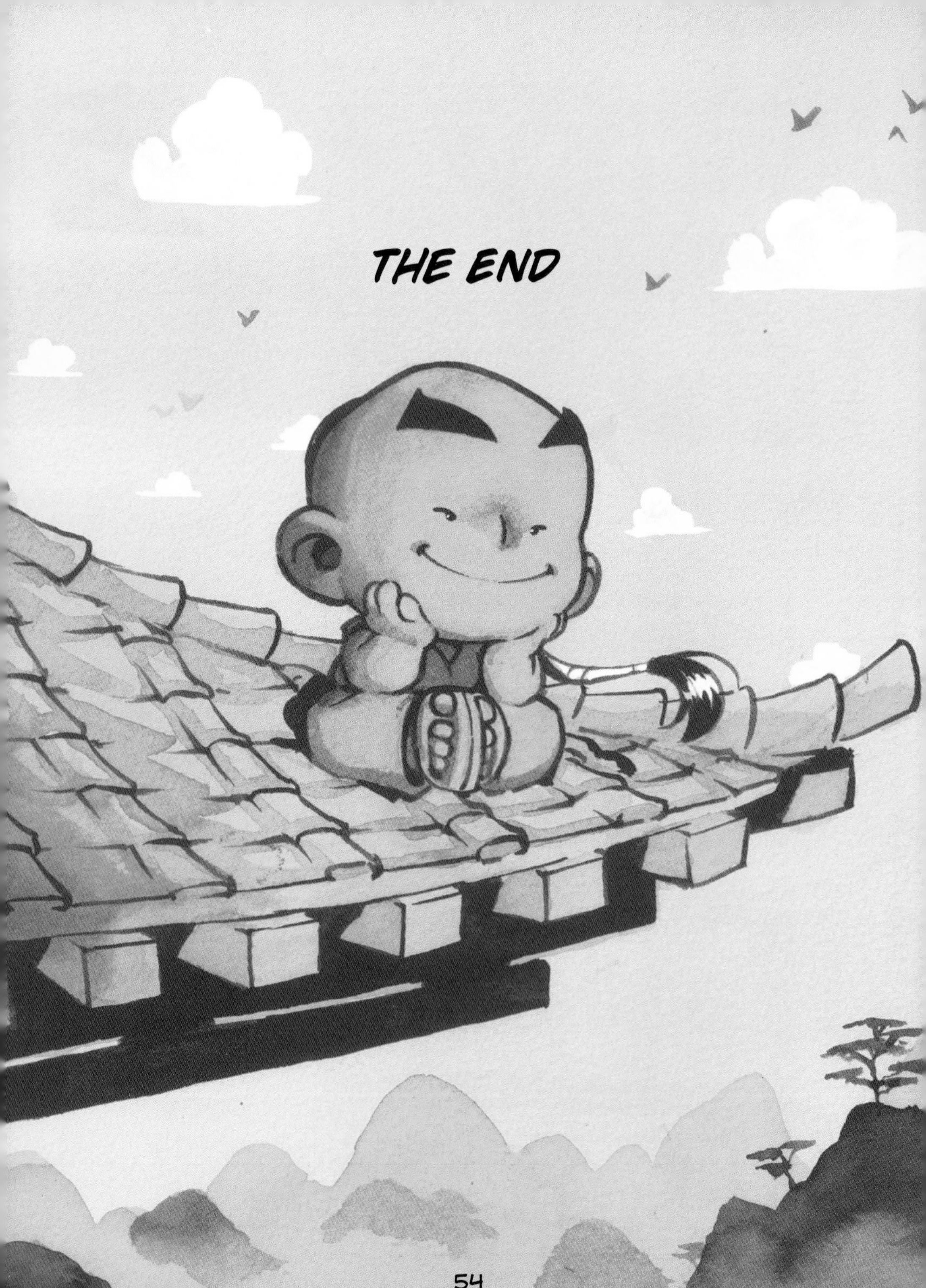
THE END

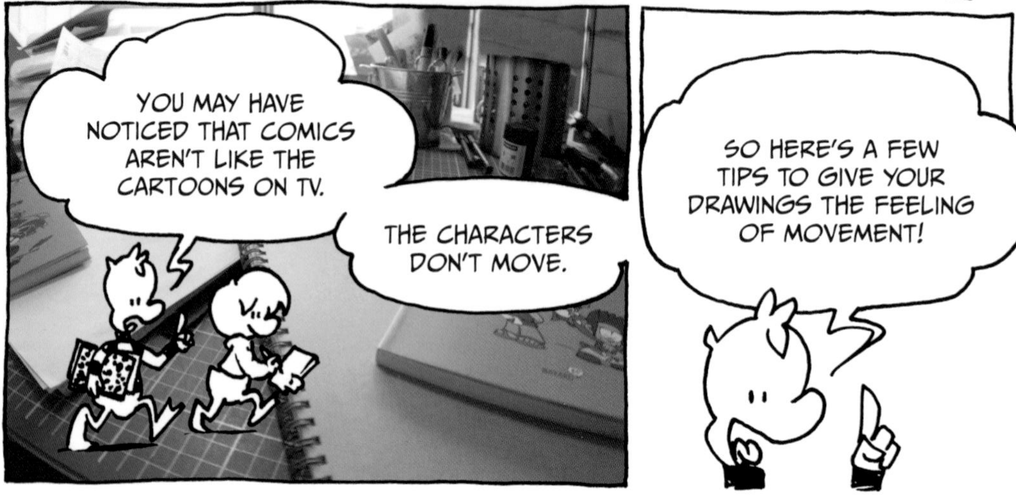
YOU MAY HAVE NOTICED THAT COMICS AREN'T LIKE THE CARTOONS ON TV.
THE CHARACTERS DON'T MOVE.
SO HERE'S A FEW TIPS TO GIVE YOUR DRAWINGS THE FEELING OF MOVEMENT!

1. Speed Lines

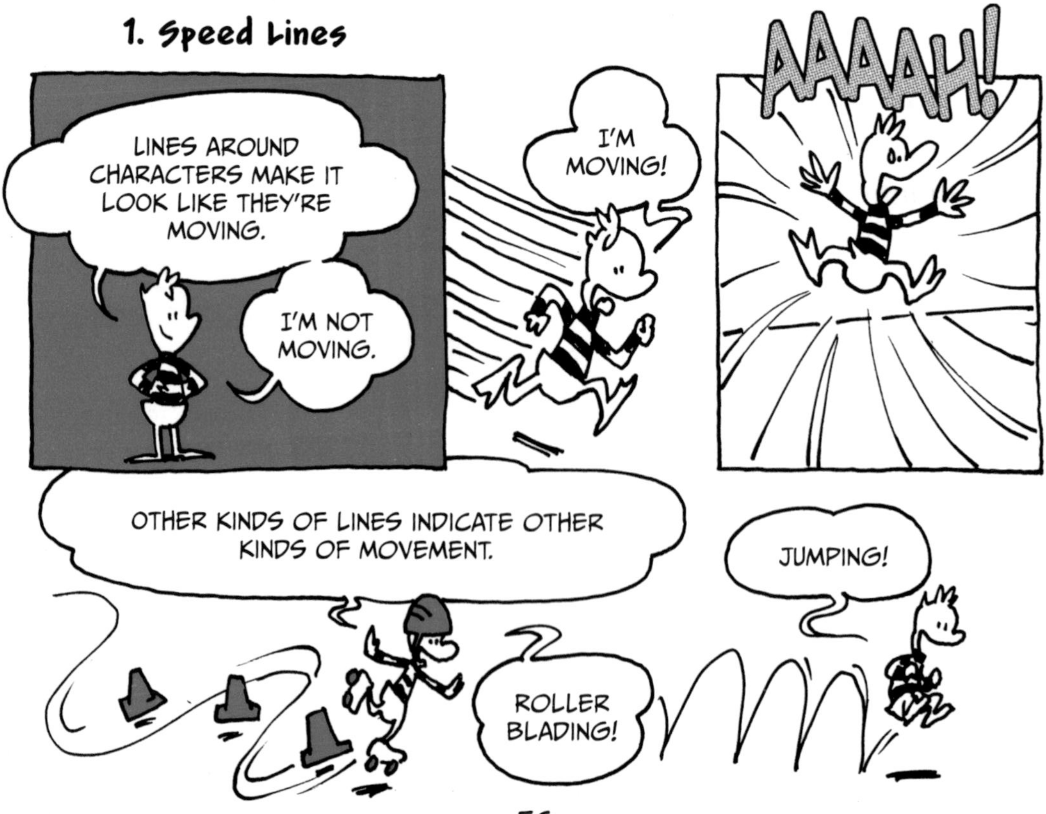
LINES AROUND CHARACTERS MAKE IT LOOK LIKE THEY'RE MOVING.
I'M NOT MOVING.
I'M MOVING!
AAAAH!
OTHER KINDS OF LINES INDICATE OTHER KINDS OF MOVEMENT.
JUMPING!
ROLLER BLADING!

2. Repetition

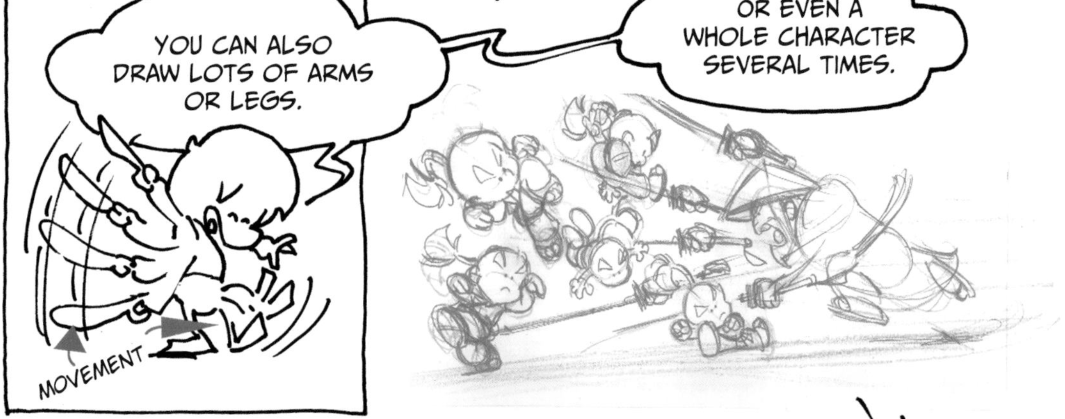
YOU CAN ALSO DRAW LOTS OF ARMS OR LEGS.
OR EVEN A WHOLE CHARACTER SEVERAL TIMES.
MOVEMENT

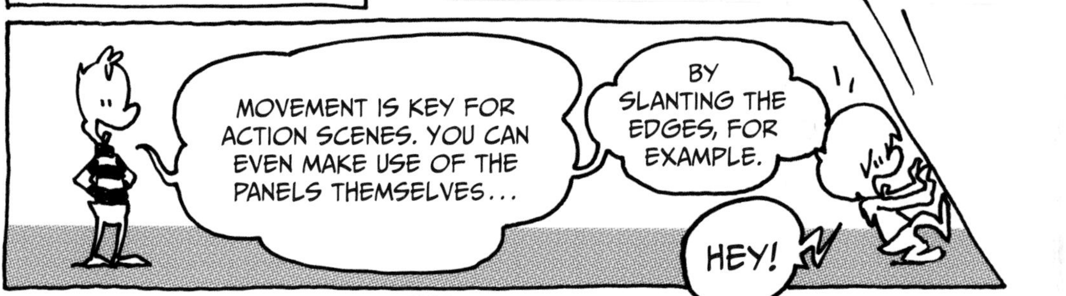
MOVEMENT IS KEY FOR ACTION SCENES. YOU CAN EVEN MAKE USE OF THE PANELS THEMSELVES...
BY SLANTING THE EDGES, FOR EXAMPLE.
HEY!

3. Layouts

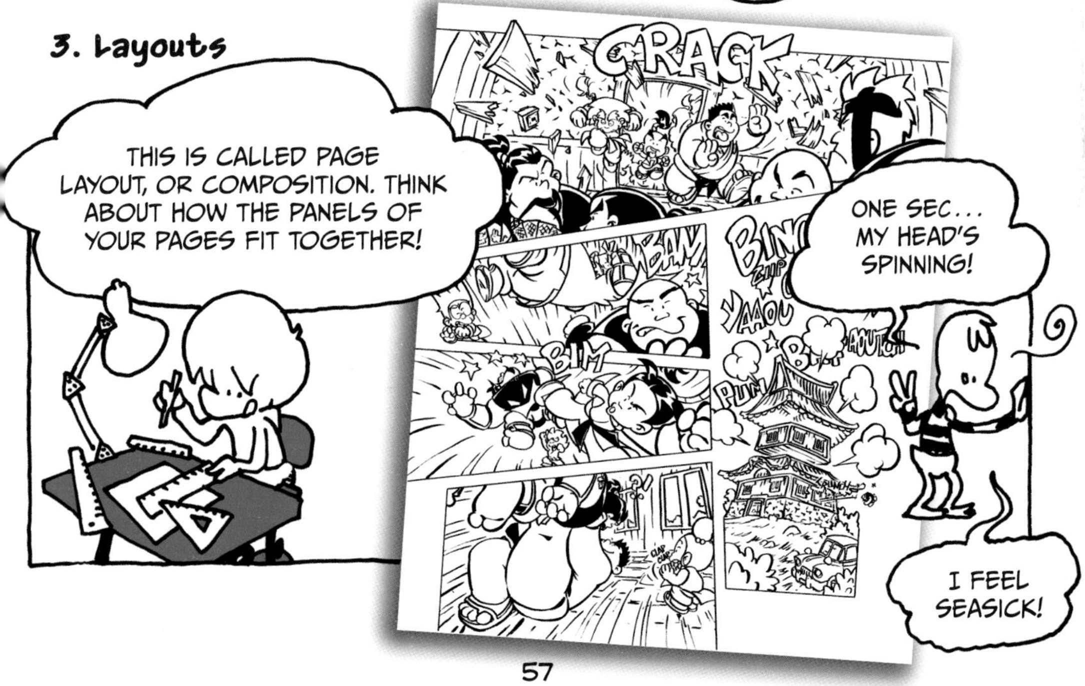
THIS IS CALLED PAGE LAYOUT, OR COMPOSITION. THINK ABOUT HOW THE PANELS OF YOUR PAGES FIT TOGETHER!
CRACK
YAAOU
ONE SEC... MY HEAD'S SPINNING!
I FEEL SEASICK!

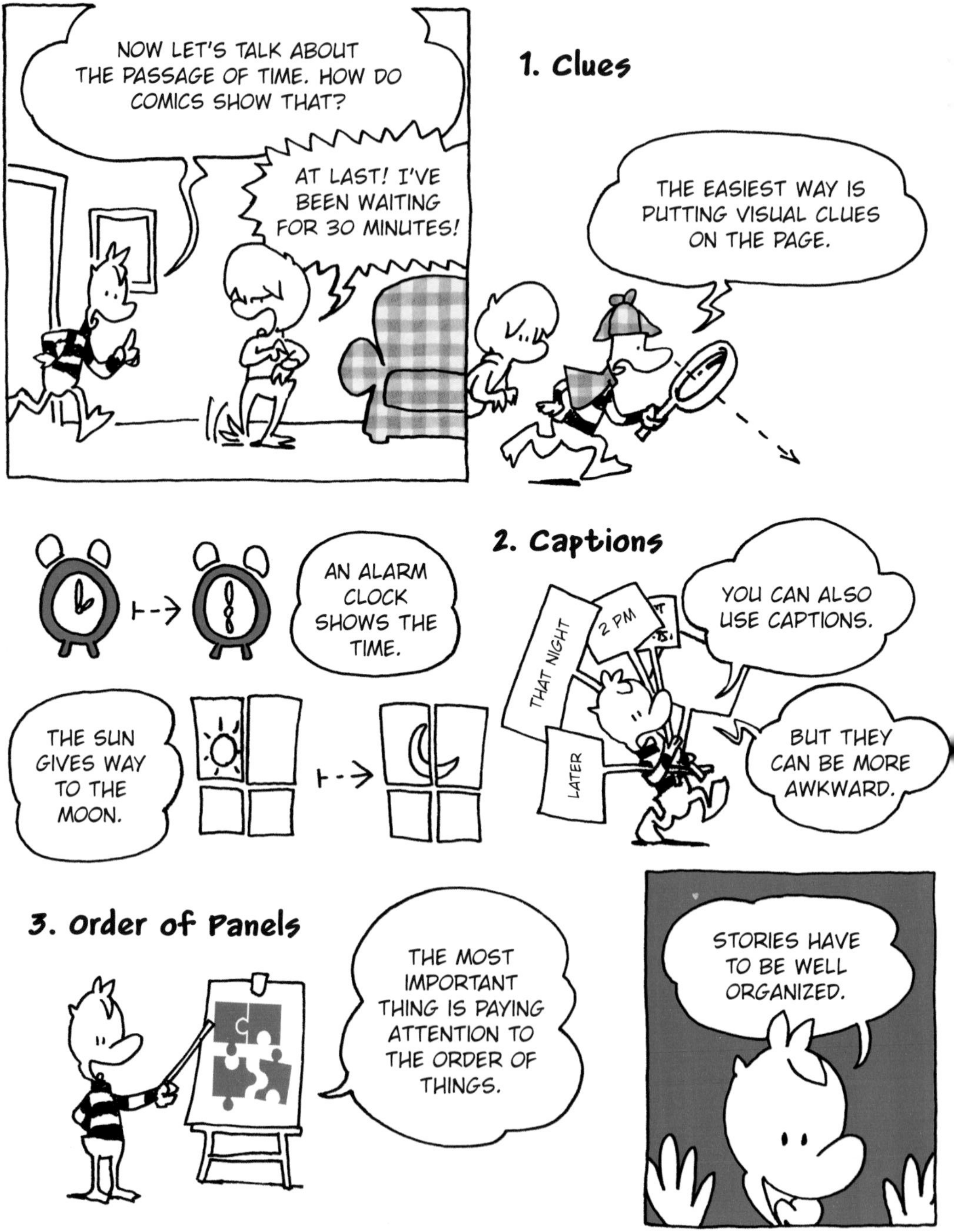
NOW LET'S TALK ABOUT THE PASSAGE OF TIME. HOW DO COMICS SHOW THAT?
AT LAST! I'VE BEEN WAITING FOR 30 MINUTES!
1. Clues
THE EASIEST WAY IS PUTTING VISUAL CLUES ON THE PAGE.
AN ALARM CLOCK SHOWS THE TIME.
THE SUN GIVES WAY TO THE MOON.
2. Captions
THAT NIGHT
2 PM
LATER
YOU CAN ALSO USE CAPTIONS.
BUT THEY CAN BE MORE AWKWARD.
3. Order of Panels
THE MOST IMPORTANT THING IS PAYING ATTENTION TO THE ORDER OF THINGS.
STORIES HAVE TO BE WELL ORGANIZED.

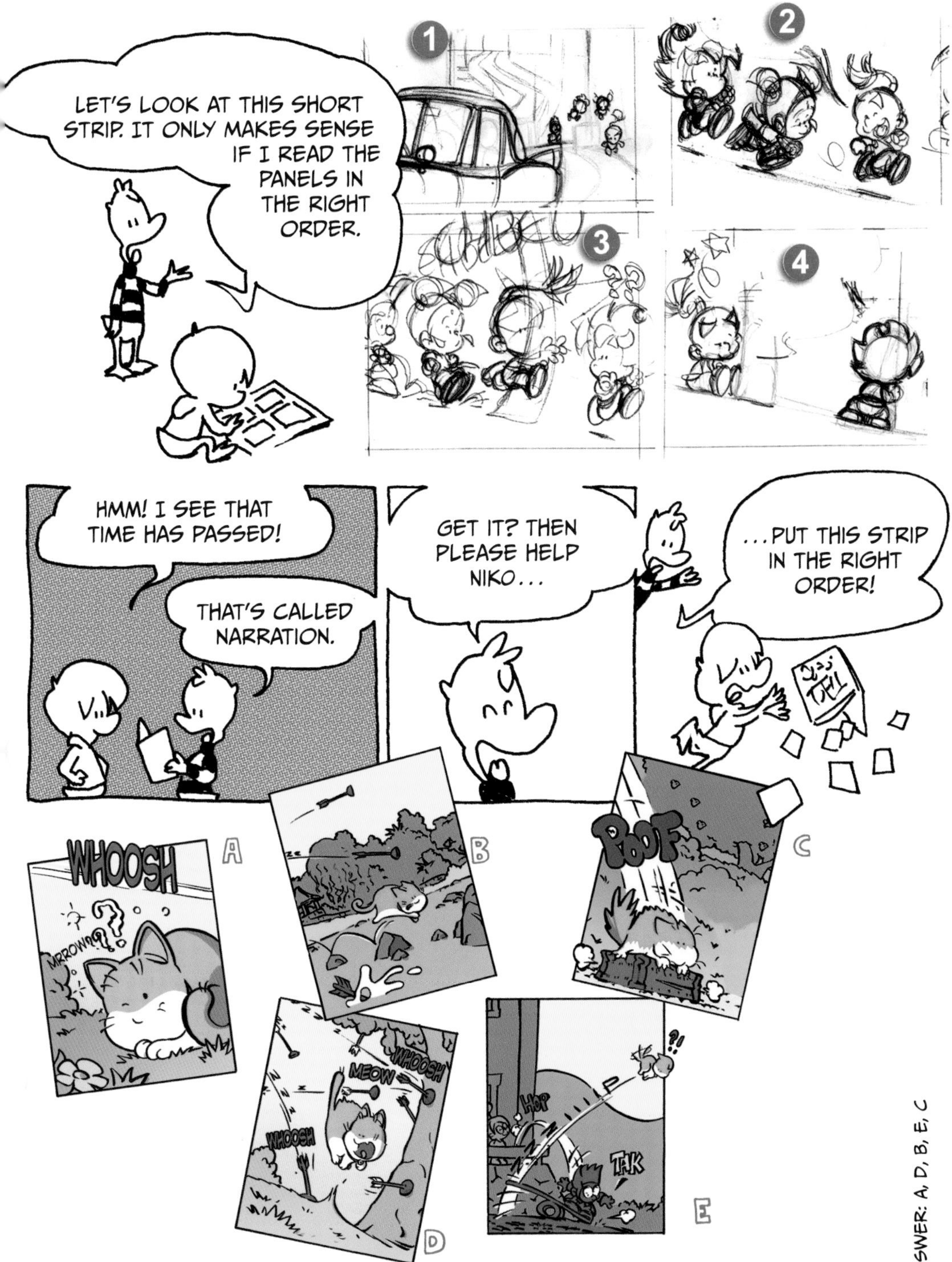

LET'S LOOK AT THIS SHORT STRIP. IT ONLY MAKES SENSE IF I READ THE PANELS IN THE RIGHT ORDER.
1
2
3
4
HMM! I SEE THAT TIME HAS PASSED!
THAT'S CALLED NARRATION.
GET IT? THEN PLEASE HELP NIKO...
...PUT THIS STRIP IN THE RIGHT ORDER!
A
WHOOSH
MRROW?
B
C
POOF
D
MEOW
WHOOSH
WHOOSH
E
HOP
?!
TAK

ANSWER: A, D, B, E, C

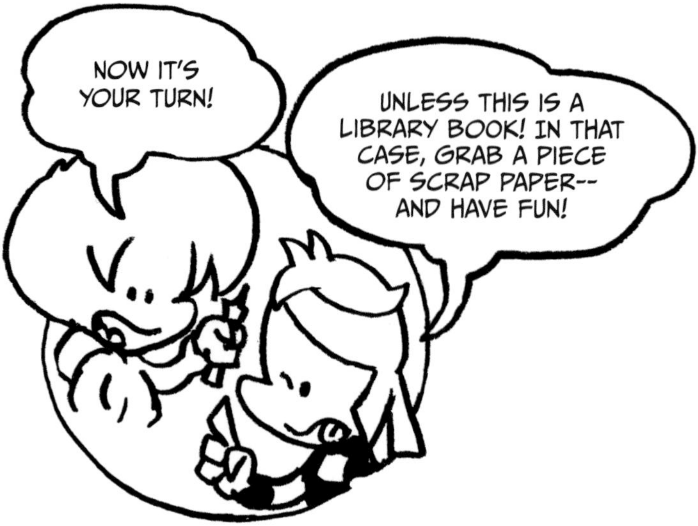
NOW IT'S YOUR TURN!
UNLESS THIS IS A LIBRARY BOOK! IN THAT CASE, GRAB A PIECE OF SCRAP PAPER-- AND HAVE FUN!

ABOUT THE AUTHOR

Laurent Richard worked in the world of advertising before becoming a professor of graphic arts. He now divides his time between teaching and illustration for children's publishing and media.

ABOUT THE ILLUSTRATOR

Nicolas Ryser attended the School of Graphic Arts Estienne in Paris. He won several competitions including the Angoulême and works for the magazine *Casus Belli*. He was recently awarded a *Graine de pro* ("Seed of a professional") prize.

TAO
The Little Samurai

#1 Pranks and Attacks!
#2 Ninjas and Knock Outs!
#3 Clowns and Dragons!
#4 The Championship!
#5 Wild Animals!

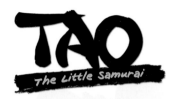

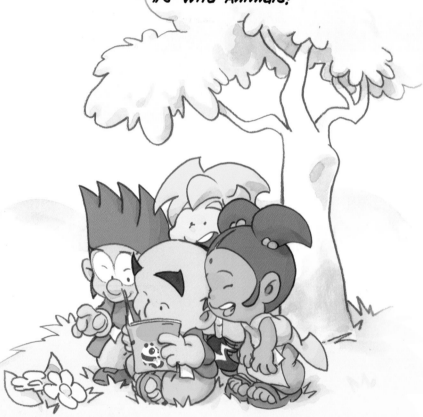